She Named You Donna

- A MEMOIR -

Julie Kerton

Paper and Prose Publishing

For my children — all of them

There is no greater agony than bearing an untold story inside you.

Maya Angelou

AUTHOR'S NOTE

I have changed the names of some of the characters to protect their identities. Some characters' names were invented as they were not fixed in my memory. I have documented places and events as accurately as possible. In some scenes, timelines were adjusted in order to move the events forward, but these adjustments do not compromise the truthfulness of the scenes or the fact that this is a true story.

CONTENTS

PART I

Adoptions, Births, Jesus and Julie

CHAPTER ONE

THERE ARE SEASONS IN LIFE that stand apart, a course for change, securely etched in memory. Autumn of 1973 was my season. I was fifteen and had just begun sophomore year at an all-girls Catholic high school. 1973, the year that the military withdrew from Vietnam; Roe v. Wade went to the Supreme Court and Watergate was the lead story on the evening news. But the most important events in my world were shared with my friends, our world no bigger than our small city thirty miles north of Manhattan. We listened to Carole King and Elton John, hid our cigarettes in our knee socks and lived on Kit Kats and TAB. And though I thought life would be like this forever, not unlike the world around me, I would soon experience shame and scandal, long for choices and hope for closure.

I get a ride to school most mornings from my neighbor. My books and purse, really a green canvas mess kit that my

3

grandfather carried during World War I, sit on the small hallway table. I'm wearing my regulation navy blue skirt to my knees, white collared blouse, blue blazer and blue knee socks with black platform shoes. I don't know how I've gotten away with the platforms, but so far no one has said anything. The horn blows as the silvery blue Mustang pulls in front. Alice is driving, she's a senior and her friend is in the bucket seat next to her. I squeeze in the back with the other riders and within seconds we are racing across town. I study Alice's moves as she simultaneously smokes, juggles a cup of coffee, pushes down on the clutch and shifts gears all with the grace and flow of a prima ballerina. I inhale the smoke as it drifts to the back seat, while we drive through the iron gates of Our Lady of Good Counsel Academy, or just Good Counsel, its unofficial name. We pass the stone chapel, final resting place for the founder of the order of nuns entombed below the altar, and a strange gray ranch style house that looks like it landed sometime around 1960. That's where the English classes are held. The buildings, except for the chapel, are not particularly pretty; most are from the turn of the century and have a haunted sort of quality, with narrow back staircases, mahogany banisters that sweep the main stairwells, wood floors, dark wainscoting and painted tin ceilings. The only other new building is the gym, where we are forced to wear something that resembles prison garb; one - piece mustard colored shorts and striped top combination, surely designed as some sort of punishment. You might say there is a mishmash quality to this school, though the grounds are beautiful with their walkways that meander under the majestic trees.

We park in the lot behind the cafeteria, and I have to run a few buildings down to my locker before the first bell. To be late means a trip to the office, which must be avoided. The nuns are what make a Catholic school a Catholic school; their expectations, intolerance for disrespect, uniformity of beliefs. For the most part, I have lived within these guidelines, but at fifteen, I feel temptation tugging at my soul. I'm much more interested in fun than in work, and I'm having a difficult time doing more than just enough.

I really do love my Religion class. It holds my attention for the entire period. This is a class like none I have experienced, and Sr. Rosemary is unlike any nun I have known. She inspires me and allows the freedom to question. Question God. One day she announced to the class, "I had a fight with Jesus last night, I was screaming at him, throwing things. It was quite an argument." My friends thought she was crazy. I thought she was deep. We had an understanding. I don't hold the same enthusiasm for Sr.

Alphonse who is determined to make my artwork her own by taking a brush to my paintings in their final stages. The Guidance Counselor is Sr. Therese. She also teaches a course on relevant topics, health, and social issues.

Sr. Therese showed a film in class that was very vague, very confusing. She kept turning the volume down and talking about being selfish and the "M word." I didn't get it until lunch when I asked the girls at my table. Eileen saw it during first period and revealed that "M" stands for masturbation and apparently it's selfish. After lunch, which usually is not much more than a yogurt and a Tab, Debbie and I leave to have a cigarette. Our school shares its campus with a college. We have figured a way to enter the dorm from behind and have claimed a small lounge, which is always empty, has two maroon couches and a coffee table. While most girls are smoking in the cafeteria bathroom and getting caught by a random check, we have a bird's eye view of any incoming nuns. At the end of the day, I meet my group of friends at my locker; Melissa, our moral compass, Debbie, whose motto is "let's have some good clean fun," Eileen the savvy one, Susan the giddy, high strung friend and Colleen who is always happy and carefree. As we walk onto North Broadway, we roll up our skirts, light up and head to downtown White Plains to catch the bus.

6

Lately I've been going to my new friend Melanie's house after school. She goes to public school and gets out before I do. As I turn onto her block, I can see her sitting on the front stoop, where she always waits for me. She's wearing her hooded blue sweat jacket with her blond hair tucked in. I follow the perfectly formed smoke rings that she has blown toward the street. Her house is like most of the houses in Prospect Park; stucco with a slate roof, a yard full of oversized bushes and a hoop that hangs over the garage door. Her parents are divorced or getting divorced and her mom works full time. Melanie's older sister and her boyfriend are always down in the basement. Their song is "Stairway to Heaven," which they turn up really loud every time it comes on the radio. Melanie and I usually just hang out in her room where Mark Spitz leers at us in his American Flag Speedo. She thinks he is really cute. I think he's gross. We sit on the floor and talk. She talks about the guys she knows. She's really worried about her friend Scott. He was hit by a car as he made his way along the Bronx River Parkway. She wants to visit him, but she thinks he's in a coma. No visitors if you're in a coma. She really wants to introduce me to her friend John one of these days. She thinks he's small

7

and cute like me. I tell her that I want my ears pierced, but my mother said I have to wait until I'm eighteen.

"I'll do it. My friend Valerie did it herself. She just used a regular sewing needle, but first you have to freeze your ear," Melanie offers.

"Okay," I say.

So we gather our supplies; ice, plastic bags for the ice, a sewing needle, matches, rubbing alcohol, toilet paper because we can't find any cotton, and a pen. Then we get her mother's jewelry box and rummage through the jewelry, most of it costume. They have to have gold posts and something I can live with until my mother notices and insists I'll need new gold studs.

"How about these?" Melanie asks as she holds up gold and emerald drop earrings.

I stare at them, then back to the others as though I'm being shown a collection at Hartsdale Jewelers.

"I guess they're not too drop," I decide as I rummage hoping that I'll find something not so fancy, something smaller.

"My mom never wears earrings anyway, she won't notice anything missing," Melanie assures me.

I take them and we go into the bathroom. We decide on where the holes should go and she carefully marks them.

While I attempt to freeze my ear, Melanie sterilizes the needle, first with the match then the alcohol.

"Now this is probably going to hurt," she warns, giving her an air of professionalism. I wince as the needle slowly pushes through my ear lobe. I try not to cry. There is no turning back. After a lot of in and out, pushing and pulling, Melanie finally gets the needle all the way through. She takes one of the emerald drop earrings and pushes it into my sore, not frozen at all, ear. Then it's on to the other side of my head. When we are done, we admire me in the bathroom mirror. I'm sure I look different, not like the girl who left for my Catholic school this morning. Melanie and I clean up and I take my books, purse and walk home, my ears stinging in the wind.

It's finally Friday night. The weather is still pretty warm, but darkness is coming earlier and earlier, making it feel later than it really is. The streetlights cast a silhouette on the trees that have near completely shed all their leaves, raked neatly to the curb. Melanie and I are meeting Susan at her cousin Cathy's house. Susan is my giddy friend from school and Cathy lives across the street from Melanie. The plan for tonight is to get drunk. I'm not sure whose idea it was, but we're all in. Melanie and I snuck orange juice, soda and cups from our houses and hid them behind a stretch of large rocks. Susan and Cathy see us walking up the driveway through the large bay window and motion us to come in. We follow them to the family room where Cathy's parents are absorbed in a card game, so it doesn't take much for Cathy to slide a bottle of vodka from the closet under her jacket. We pause in front of the console television to see President Nixon nominating Gerald Ford as Vice President and watch long enough to look interested, say goodnight, then try to contain ourselves as we make our way out the front door. Fleeing across the yard and down the street, we stop just briefly to fetch our stash.

Melanie, giggling, looks at Cathy and says, "I can't believe you did that!"

"Oh, my God that was amazing," I add.

Susan leads the way down the road, looking for a place that isn't lit by streetlights and out of view of passersby. She finds us a spot tucked behind thick bushes, lined by a split rail fence at the edge of a dark lot. Cathy carefully takes the bottle out from her jacket as Melanie and I unpack our bags and set the assorted goods down on a flat section of grass. I hand out the cups as Cathy pours the vodka.

"What do you guys want in it, soda or orange juice?" Melanie asks.

"Orange juice," we all agree.

I like the way it tastes and the slow burn it leaves down my throat. I drink quickly and already want a refill.

"More orange juice than vodka, and don't drink so fast," Melanie reminds me.

This is my first time drinking, so Melanie is looking out for me tonight.

We've drunk all we possibly can and leave the remnants of our party in a patch of pachysandra then wander through the streets of White Plains. Passing an enormous pile of leaves, we jump in without a thought. We slowly sink to the bottom and come up for air, then do it again and again, finally resting on a soft pillow of foliage. Looking up at the sky we talk about school and the people we know. The subject turns to guys and all of a sudden we are talking about French kissing, first base, second, third and going all the way. I'm feeling a little dizzy when Melanie mentions B.J.'s, as Susan and Cathy shout out in repulsion. I think I know, but I'm not positive what B.J. stands for, so I'll ask my savvy friend, Eileen, when I see her in school on Monday. We brush the leaves off and walk toward Highlands Junior High School's parking lot.

At the end of the night, Melanie and I carefully teeter back to my house, hanging on to each other, giggling as we try to balance. We pass the driveway, and I can see my mother in front of the hedges with our Irish Wolf-hound, Butch.

"Hi Mom," I yell, "thizz is my sister, Melanie, oops, I mean my friend, Melanie," I giggle.

"Hi Melanie, it's nice to finally meet you. Did you girls have fun tonight?" my mother asks in a cheerful voice.

"Mmmm, hmmm," Melanie and I say as steadily and seriously as possible.

We pet Butch before my mother brings him into the house. Once my mother closes the door we fall to the ground in a fit of laughter, positive that introducing Melanie as my sister, is the funniest thing that has ever happened. In my haze I'm not surprised my mother didn't seem to notice. I'm sure my mother has had her usual two, maybe three, scotch and waters by now. That usually takes care of her noticing too much about me. Finally standing, we hold each other up, then carefully turn and go our separate ways.

"I'll call you tomorrow," Melanie shouts from the street as I make my way up the cement stairs. I push open the door and find the couch in the living room.

The next morning I crack my eyes open against their protest. I'm still in my blue jeans and striped turtleneck

12

from the night before. My body is hot and sweaty and my head, my head is pounding. I put my hands over my ears to silence the painful and exaggerated sound coming from the kitchen. My father is opening ice trays and directing my brother to the location of the folding table. Then I remember. West Point. Army. Football. Tailgate. No, not today. I hurry through the kitchen, past my father, past my brother, slide into the bathroom, promising myself that I will never drink again.

———

Most Sunday mornings, Melanie and I make the church rounds together. My church is St. Bernard's, and I'm expected to attend every Sunday, no matter what. Melanie goes to the Highlands Church. I've convinced my parents that we are going to both churches to open our minds to other people's faith. Instead we go to the diner and share an order of fries. As Melanie soaks the fries in ketchup, I ask her about Scott. I've thought about him from the time she first told me about his accident. Hit by a car, on a highway, barely survived, maybe he won't. She finally visited him in the hospital the other day.

"He didn't look too good, part of his hair was shaved off, and he was hooked up to a bunch of tubes and wires.

But we were talking and joking, so I think he's going to be okay," she says.

I feel relieved to hear this. I've wondered about him. Wondered if he would die. I'm not sure why I should care, but I do.

"What does he look like normally, I mean what does his hair look like usually?" I ask.

"Hmm, kind of dirty blonde, light brownish sort of, not too long," she says.

"How tall is he, you know is he tall or short?" I continue quizzing.

"Oh, he's pretty tall, maybe six feet?" she guesses.

"I was just wondering," I say, not letting on that he has preoccupied a good deal of space in my thoughts lately. I knew he must be strong, and now I know he's strong, tall and has dirty blonde hair. I take another fry as Melanie tells me that she's thinking about getting her hair cut, and I'm trying to imagine what Scott looks like.

Before we get home, we stop at Melanie's Protestant Church, a beautiful stone building with stained glass set kitty corner on the property, making it appear especially holy. We enter through the heavy wood door on the side and take a bulletin off the table, and then walk the few blocks down to St. Bernard's that sits in the middle of a block of houses, set close to the sidewalk. It's not imposing, rather there is an unusual simplicity in its Italian style, with a mix of stone and brick, and a wide steep staircase with wrought iron handles ascending up to the Corinthian columns and arches that frame the doorway. The bulletins are on a table just past the holy water, where I always stop to bless myself. I'm sure that counts for something. We part ways at the top of my street, and I promise I'll call her later.

It's hot in the Spanish Lab. The afternoon sun pours into the large windows and the ancient radiators hiss steam and gurgle as they warm the water inside them. Most of us have tossed our blazers and sweaters on the back of our chairs, our knee socks rolled to our ankles, blouses un-tucked with the sleeves rolled up. It's eighth period and I'm getting nervous about meeting Melanie and her friends, John and Tim. I wasn't nervous until now, because the day felt like it would never end. When the bell rings, I grab my books and quickly head toward the stairs, hoping to avoid the end of the day gridlock. We are meeting at Gedney Way, a street with a small row of stores, so I'll have to take the Scarsdale bus and run a few extra blocks. I'm out of breath and just make it in time to count out thirty-five cents when the bus pulls up. I find an empty seat toward the back and stare out the window. I'm beginning to wish that I hadn't agreed to meet them. I'm not exactly sure what we are going to do. Maybe just walk around a while. When I see the fire station, I pull the cord to alert the driver, and the bus stops at the corner. I spot Melanie waving across the street.

"Julie, this is John and Tim," Melanie says.

"Hi," I reply, not looking directly at anyone.

"Hey what's up," says John with a smile that demands attention and forces me to look right into his eyes. I think he kind of looks like a little John Denver, but without glasses.

We all start to walk to the deli where we each buy a soda and cross the street toward the woods. There is a railing at the head of the trail, so I hold my uniform skirt down as I throw one leg over at a time, trying not to drop my books and soda. The leaves crunch under our feet and we hold the branches back as we walk further and further, stopping a few feet from the edge of a brook and sit on the leaf-covered ground.

"Do you guys want to smoke?" John asks.

Melanie and Tim say, "sure."

I don't say anything. Melanie turns on her radio as John takes out a plastic bag of pot and rolling papers from his oversized green army jacket. I know that you can buy rolling paper and pipes at a cramped store downtown called "Oriental." I've only bought incense there, but I've studied their variety of drug paraphernalia. I recognize the rolling paper package as John skillfully takes one out, makes a crease down the center and pours just the right amount of pot before he rolls it through his fingers, sealing it with the tip of his tongue and finally twisting the ends. He lights it and the smoke drifts around us, leaving a scent of a roasted crushed leaf that is somehow pungent and sweet at the same time. John takes a long drag, holds it in as he passes it to me. I really didn't want to be next. I was hoping he would pass it the other way, and I would have a chance to watch everyone. So I just try to do what he did. I take a long drag and hold it in. I can feel my lungs burning and my eyes tearing and I want to exhale, but I don't. I have to hold it in as I pass it to Melanie. I finally begin to exhale slowly and cough and cough some more. The joint continues around and around, getting smaller and smaller and easier and easier and I'm getting higher and higher.

My mouth feels dry, so I take a sip of soda and say, "wow this is really bubbly and wet."

Melanie, giving me a grin says, "Julie you're really stoned."

"Yeah, I think I am," I agree.

We both laugh and try to drink our sodas but we can't swallow and just sort of spit it out, making us laugh even more. Until we finally give up.

"Okay, okay, stop," I say.

John is next to me playing air guitar, I think to Jimi Hendrix. But I'm not really watching because I know I'll laugh, and I'm already laughing too much. I look around at the trees that are swaying as they tower overhead, too enchanting to ignore. The air has become weighty with layers of a smoky haze. I take another sip, this time I don't spit it out, but I feel it tingle as I swallow. When I put the can down, I look over at Melanie and Tim making out. Does this mean I have to make out with John? I can feel him moving closer to me and before I have time to think about it our lips are locked together. I'm trying to decide if I like it or not when I start thinking about Ringo because "Your Sixteen" is playing on the radio and then I'm thinking about the other Beatles when I feel John's tongue sliding around my tongue, making its way toward my throat, forcing me to breathe through my nose. We slowly fall back attached to each other by some sort of invisible force. My hands are frozen by my side, I feel his hands rubbing up and down on my bare legs. I try to stay with it, but I really don't think I can breathe and then I think I should do something with my hands, but I don't know what, so, still attached, I sit up, take a sip of soda and ask if he wants any.

"No thanks," he says. "Hey what bands do you like?"

"Um I, I don't know, I guess the Rolling Stones, how about you?" I ask.

He smiles and I giggle. I'm pretty sure we are not going to do that again, but I think we just became friends.

CHAPTER TWO

PURPLE AND WHITE CROCUSES are peaking through the small patch of brown grass around the brick wall, where John and I sit, sharing a Marlboro. Today we are meeting, his friends, Richard and Scott at Richard's apartment building on Davis Avenue. Scott left the hospital several weeks ago, and I've been curious about him since Melanie first told me about his accident. I can hear two voices coming from the street; one much sharper and clearer than the other. So I jump down and stomp out the cigarette on the pavement. The sharp, clear voice, wearing a pair of PRO-Keds, stops in front of me.

"Hey Scott, this is Julie," John says.

My eyes climb up to his face then rest in his blue eyes. And suddenly I am shy, ready to hide, but I pick up my books and purse and follow everyone.

Richard doesn't have his key, so we have to be buzzed in. We ride the elevator to the fifth floor. Once in the apartment, I browse the living room with its white walls and beige furniture. There is a slightly overweight, long haired, barefoot guy playing guitar. I think he is Richard's brother, but I don't ask as we make our way to the bedroom. I sit at the corner of the bed and put my things behind me. The shades are drawn, and there is a small dim light on the desk disguising the mess, giving it a bluish glow. John takes out a joint and lights it. He passes it to me, and I pass it to Scott and watch him as he takes it from me. It goes around a few times and when I hand him the joint this time, he looks back at me, at first in a way I don't understand and then in a way I do. I try to look away, but I don't and neither does he.

———

It isn't long before Scott is waiting for me at the end of each day by the school gates. We walk downtown and sit on a bench to talk and watch the people go by. He usually has something funny to say, and I always laugh. Of course we talk about serious things, too. I can talk to Scott about anything. Some days we go to my house, when I have to be there for my younger brothers and sister, while my mother is working. Scott is friendly and animated and my siblings like when he's there. Left alone we don't kiss or touch, not yet. I'm wrapped in emotions that I don't recognize. My body stirred with sensations that are unfamiliar.

Today we are hanging out at Scott's house, in his room. His bedroom is really a sunroom off the living room, surrounded by windows with moss green curtains and a matching bedspread. There is a chest of draws and not much room for anything else other than the small desk. It's understood that the door should be left open. His grandmother is at the house watching his younger sister today. Scott is showing me pictures of when he went to Wyoming and describes the mountains, the vastness, painting a picture of its beauty.

"I want to go there someday," I tell him.

"Yeah, you'd really love it. Hey maybe we can go together," he says.

I watch him as he puts the pictures back on the dresser, and suddenly an ache washes over me. These feelings rise up in me more often now, and I think they also do in him. We are trying not to touch, but we do and there is a passion that can't be calmed. My body shivers with anticipation as he pushes me down and lies next to me. Our hands begin to explore, and I can feel his body trembling with mine. He stops and reaches over to shut the door, then locks it, and we both know what is going to happen. We kiss wildly and he lifts my shirt pulling at my bra, his hands skim my body from my neck to my stomach and back up again. I touch him clumsily, and think we should stop, but I don't want to. He's struggling with my zipper and now his. I wiggle my sneakers off and slide down my underwear and pants. He's doing the same. He lies on top of me, as I spread my legs apart, his fingers searching, my fingers searching. He's trying to push inside of me, but he is sliding back and forth and side to side. I don't think this is going to work, but Scott pushes again, this time with more force making me scream out in pain. I didn't know it was going to hurt. He covers my mouth to muffle the sound as he pushes his body up then down, up and down over and over. My screams subside, so he takes his hands away. I watch him as he thrusts faster and stronger making the bed bang against the wall. His face is turning red and twisting, his eyes are shut tight, and I think he's going to explode. He lets out a noise that I've never heard before and collapses on top of me.

———————

I hide the birth control pills in a purse that hangs in the back of my closet. I went to Planned Parenthood the day after Scott and I lost our virginity. I was given a white disc with twenty-eight pills. The nurse instructed me on when to start taking them and went over the possible side effects. "There can be no intercourse until you get your next period," she explained, as I looked down, embarrassed. I take one every night. I never forget. I'm very responsible. In fact, I have always been responsible, driven by the values instilled by my parents and the Church. But now I also have to be responsible for the part of me that is swirling with desire and dizzied by love. So as the spring disappears into summer, Scott and I are together all the time. Days run into nights, so I make sure to never forget.

A couple of weeks ago we were walking through a rainstorm. As we turned into my driveway, he pulled my arm to stop me. With the trees sheltering us, he handed me a small black velvet box and said, "I wanted to give you your birthday present a little early."

"Oh my God, okay."

This was the first present he had given me, so it felt a little awkward, but I took the delicate gold ring out of the box, slipped it on and knew I would wear it forever.

———

We spend most of our time at my house. It's old and white with brown trim, three floors, and two large porches. My mother and I think the house is haunted, but I'm not afraid of the ghost who visits; I think she may linger in the dumbwaiter that runs through my closet. I'm on babysitting duty until my mother gets home, which is usually around the middle of the afternoon. After that, Scott and I get lost in the rooms that nobody uses. The third floor has an enormous room with alcoves, where we can tuck ourselves away. My mother never goes up those stairs or down to the basement. That's where Scott and I play pool and smoke pot in the rain cellar, then have sex on one of the couches. We've also discovered that we can hang off the second floor porch railing to smoke pot. The smell goes up and out. I've learned that Scott takes other drugs. He introduced me to acid recently, and I trusted him when he said I would like it, that is was fun. But I have too many responsibilities to find it fun. Like the day my brother fell off his bike and was badly cut. I had to figure out how to clean the cut and wrap it with a bandage. It took much too long, with blood spewing everywhere. In the end, my brother wrapped it himself. Then there was the day my mother came home early, just moments after we had taken our hits. A few short hours later, she asked me to empty the dishwasher, so while picking through the glasses and plates, I froze with confusion. Scott and I dropped acid this afternoon, and it still hasn't worn off.

"Julie, it's late, Scott has to go home now and you should get to bed," my mother yells from the top of the stairs.

Scott tells me not to worry that I'll be fine. I go up to my room and put on my nightgown with the three bears on it, get into bed and turn off the light. There are tiny dots in front of my eyes, and the darkness is smothering me. I turn the light back on and suddenly the ceiling is moving closer and closer. Escaping my bedroom I go back downstairs, where I walk down the hallway to the kitchen, then the dining room, across the center hall to the living room and into the family room, back to the kitchen, on and on, again and again, hour after hour. All this makes me think I may want to die tonight. So, I walk up the stairs to the ugly bathroom at the top of the landing, with green tile and two sinks. No one is quite sure why there are two sinks, they don't match, one doesn't work and they are on different walls. The medicine cabinet is over the sink that doesn't work. I find a razor blade, take it out of its cardboard covering and hold it carefully between two fingers. When I close the cabinet, I catch myself in the mirror and study my face; my eyes, my nose, my forehead. I watch myself, watching me. I close my eyes and when I open them, I am still holding the blade. I had forgotten that I wanted to die tonight. I step back and slide to the floor, tucking my knees under my nightgown, I notice the bears and think that they are smiling at me. "Are you talking to me?" I'm talking to the bears on my nightgown. And I begin to laugh. When the laughing stops, I look at the blade and place it on my left wrist. I hold it there for a long while and think about slicing it. I could go to sleep and then I could rest. I look down at the bears again. I like this nightgown. It's my favorite. I don't want to die tonight. I'll be okay. Scott said I'd be okay. I put the blade down; go down the stairs to the hallway, into the kitchen, then the dining room, across the center hall, on and on, again and again, hour after hour.

I'm on the darker side of life now with Scott. I was on the outside looking in, but now I'm on the inside. I thought I'd like it here. Sometimes I wish I was still the girl who wore her bear nightgown and kissed her parents goodnight and went to bed. But then I remember, with Scott it's fun. But I'm beginning to think it's no fun at all.

———————

I rouse from an unrestricted summer to the ruled and regulated days of September. I get my locker number and see my friends and the giggling and gossip picks up as usual. I like the order of school. I don't really mind wearing a uniform. I don't have to think about it. I'm happy to be back at school. Scott is having a harder time getting back to the reality of homework and curfews. It is difficult for him to pull away from me.

I'm in math class when my friend Colleen asks, "Julie is that Scott standing over there?" I look out the window across the grounds and see him leaning in the doorway of the college. I recognize his stance, his plaid shirt and light brown hair covering his face. When class is over I walk to the side of the building and motion him to meet me around the back. I don't want to get caught. He doesn't care about getting caught. But I do.

"What are you doing here?" I hurriedly ask.

"I thought you might want to leave early and we can go somewhere," he says as he lights a cigarette.

"I can't," I say, my voice high and squeaky. "You better go, this is not good, I'll see you later, okay? I'm sorry."

Scott doesn't understand that I know people have seen us. I know that I will be called to the office to have a talk with Sr. Rita, the Assistant Principal. Maybe I shouldn't have gone over to him, but then he may have come closer. I listen to the end of the day announcements. Shit, I've been called to the office. My palms are sweaty, legs weak, heart racing as I climb the stairs to the office. This is my second visit to Sr. Rita's office. Last June we discussed the red mark on my neck and although I tried to think of some way to explain it, we both knew how it got there. I was warned not to continue with that behavior, and I promised it would never happen again. Her door always ajar, I knock lightly.

"Julie, come in," Sr. Rita says.

Now I'm standing in the small cramped office. The two windows dwarf the room but don't bring in any light. The dark brown carpet is a sharp contrast to the orange carpet just outside her door. The small table in the corner is cluttered with paper, and books are stacked on the chairs around it. Sitting at her desk, just below the crucifix, she blends in with her black habit and brown sweater. Her eyes are affixed to mine and her face does not look pleased.

"I was told you were seen with a boy by the college entrance during school hours. Is that true?" she asks.

"Yes Sister, but I didn't know he was coming, I told him he wasn't allowed," I say, my eyes now cast toward the floor.

"Is he your boyfriend?" she continues.

"Umm kind of, but I didn't know he was coming here, Sister. I told him never to come again," I restate, praying she will lessen the penance she has in mind.

"Shouldn't he be in school today?" she asks.

"Yes Sister," I say.

"Where does he go to school?" she asks

30

"He goes to the high school, White Plains," I answer.

"I don't know why he wasn't in school; I don't know why he came here. I just told him he wasn't allowed here," I continue.

"You know if this happens again there will be consequences. Be careful Julie," she says.

"Yes Sister. Thank you Sister, I'm sorry, Sister," I say as I back out of the office with a sense of relief and appreciation.

———————

Scott had to go live with his father after Christmas. His mother sent him. He wasn't going to school much. I wish Scott liked school. I know he's smart, but he would rather hang out. I think he may be doing more drugs. There was always arguing and yelling when he was home. He hates his stepfather and is really angry with his mother for marrying him. He doesn't talk too much about his father, but he did tell me about the day his father left his family. Scott tried to hold his truck as he backed out of their driveway. He begged him not to leave. Then he chased the truck down the street until it turned the corner.

Now Scott and his father live together in a garden apartment about a half hour up the Taconic Parkway. Scott sleeps in the spare bedroom. He called me the other night. When I heard the phone ring, I ran to it, yelling, "I'll get it!" Most times I'm really disappointed, but this time it was Scott. My heart beat faster and I smiled in relief, when I heard his voice on the other end of the line.

I told him how much I missed him then asked, "are you coming to White Plains soon? Or can I come up there?"

He didn't answer me, and I knew something was wrong. I opened the basement door, pulled the phone cord and sat on the cold wood steps.

"Is everything alright?" I asked, not really wanting to know.

A long stretch of quiet hung over us until he said something that sounded like we probably shouldn't see each other anymore. Numbness enveloped me.

"Why are you saying this?" I asked. "I love you. You gave me a ring, please. What did I do?"

Scott told me I didn't do anything that we just should break up and then hung up without saying goodbye, leaving me listening to dead air. Then a sick crying stirred. The kind that chokes. I got up off the stairs and hung the phone up on the wall.

"What's wrong?" my father asked patting the couch, "ah, come here."

He slid me under his arm as I used his shirt to wipe my nose and cheeks.

Through fierce sobs I tried to say, "Scott broke up with me."

"I'm sorry, I knew this had to happen sometime. It'll be all right," he told me.

And we sat together for a long, long time.

———————

I can't seem to fill in the space of Scott. With him I was exciting and wild, even reckless. Alone, I'm plain, just another girl, nothing special. There is no more color. It's gone. I walk through the routines that are in place. After dinner, I do homework; wash my hair, but I don't take birth control pills anymore. The night Scott broke up with me, I went to the closet, took down the purse, pulled out the packet of pills, walked down the hallway to the bathroom, threw them in the toilet then flushed. I'm never having sex again. Never again.

———————

Friday afternoon. Another weekend is here. I'm not sure what I'm doing yet. I'll probably go out with Debbie. Maybe we'll see Colleen. I search the kitchen for something to munch on. I decide on an apple. Taking the first bite, the phone rings and I answer.

"Julie?"

"Yeah."

"Hey, it's Scott."

"Hi."

"I'm at my mother's house this weekend, can I see you? Can you come over?"

"Yeah sure, when?"

"Now?"

"Now, umm yeah, okay."

"Okay I'll see you soon then."

"Okay."

"Bye."

Click.

I wear the purple sweater that I really like. My mother tells me how nice I look when I ask her if I can have the car for a few hours. Of course I don't tell her where I'm really going, she'd have a million questions, and I don't have any answers. It turns out that she needs the car, so instead of driving I walk the several blocks, which gives me time to think about what I'm doing.

The buds on the trees are opening up, sprinkling the ground with bright green confetti. I love it best when the trees are in this state. It reminds me of last year when Scott would walk me home and the world looked so beautiful. I try not to get my hopes up. It's been a few months, and I've only recently stopped thinking about him every time I'm out with my friends. They made me go to a dance with them shortly after we broke up, and I spent the entire night miserable, especially when some guy asked me to dance. I didn't know how to say no, so I found myself following him. Halfway to the dance floor, I turned around and walked away. I think I should protect myself, I have to be very careful. It hurt too much. And now I think I'm finally over him. Well, I'm almost over him. That is until he opens the door and stands on the stoop wearing a navy blue sweater; his hair longer and lighter as the sun catches it, and watches me as I walk up the driveway. When I reach him, he hugs me with all his strength, burying me in his chest. Then we kiss and we don't stop kissing, we don't stop at anything. Somewhere in the middle of kissing and not stopping at anything, he tells me that his father made him break up with me. He didn't want to say any of those things, but his father was on the other line. His father can be crazy and he's afraid of him. And so we are back in his bedroom that's really a sunroom that suddenly feels like heaven.

——— — —

I put my ring back on and I'll start taking birth control pills again, as soon as I get my period. Scott and I were together that weekend when he called me. We are waiting, waiting until it's safe. I'm sure I'm going to get my period any day now. Probably today. This is my fourth trip to the bathroom this morning. I check my underwear for any possible trace of blood. I was sure that this time I'd get it. I thought I had felt something. I flush the toilet, go to the sink, wash my hands and pick up my books that I left on the windowsill. I catch up with my friends, and try to blend in and put away any worries.

"So, how are you and Scott doing? Colleen asks.

"Great. Well except I can't talk to him that much, but I think he's coming down this weekend," I say.

I try to get home as soon as I can to call Scott. I want to ask him about this weekend and see if he is still coming. His father is always around and usually won't let him talk to me. Lying on my parents' bed, I am relieved to hear his voice. He tells me he's not sure about this weekend. He has to get a ride. He hates living with his father, but right now there isn't much he can do. I twirl the phone cord as I talk to him and think about telling him I'm a couple of weeks late. But I know I'm going to get it any minute so I hold off. "I love

36

you," he tells me and he'll try to call me later. I go downstairs and get something to eat and bring it to my room, then go into the bathroom and check again. Scott calls later that night. He can only talk for a few minutes.

"I'm late."

"What?"

"I wasn't going to tell you. I'm sure I'm going to get my period tomorrow."

"How late?"

"Um, about two weeks, maybe three."

"Oh, shit."

"No, it's okay. I'm sure I'm not pregnant, I feel like I'm going to get my period, any minute."

"What are we going to do?"

"I knew I shouldn't have told you. It's fine, don't worry."

"Hey I gotta go now. I'll talk to you later."

"Okay, it will be fine really, I'm sorry I told you, please don't worry. I love you."

Late in the afternoon, the following day I leap to the phone when it rings. "Hello," I answer practically out of breath. This time I wish I hadn't answered. It's Scott's father. He knows. He knows I may be pregnant. He probably was on the other line when I spoke to Scott. He wants me to stop by his construction site at the hospital tomorrow after school, around 4:30. He'll be at the corner of Maple and South Lexington. I agree to meet him. He tells me not to mention it to Scott. I agree to that too. I'll agree to anything, so I can hang up the phone.

Lockers slam as the day comes to an end. It's particularly loud and always bothers me. The ceilings are low and the room is really cramped. I'm usually out the door and on my way within moments, but today I'm taking my time. I carefully check my black and white notebook for assignments and the list of books I need. We're reading "Member of the Wedding," and I always have math homework, so I'll need that textbook too, and my Spanish book, social studies and large binder. I stack the books largest to smallest and hug them in front of me, hang my green canvas bag over my shoulder, walk down the few steps to the back door and take a deep breath of fresh air and sigh. I have to meet Scott's father in about an hour. I think I'll stop and get a soda first. I'm too nervous to eat anything. I'm not going to let myself think about how strange this meeting is. I'm just a little late getting my period. I can't talk to Scott's father about it. I can't believe he knows. I can't believe he listens to Scott and me on the phone. I hope Scott's okay. I wish I could have talked to him after his father called me.

My mouth feels dusty. I finished the soda blocks ago, and I have a lump in my throat. As I approach the hospital, on South Lexington, I see Scott's father waiting for me, and I look down toward the pavement.

"Hello Julie, how are you?" he asks.

"Fine, thank you," I answer.

"Uh, well, I understand that you and Scott may be in some trouble," he says.

"I guess so, maybe, I'm not sure," I answer, struck by the late afternoon sun, lighting a golden blaze on the construction site. Stone and brick have been attached to the main building and a structure is emerging.

"You know this could ruin both of your lives. You know that. Right?" he continues.

"Hmm hmm," I say absently, my attention toward the trucks and machines, which I had expected to be working, lifting the dirt, moving the stones into place.

"Uh, I can help you. You could have an abortion. No one will ever have to know," he offers.

I look at Scott's father, but I'm listening to the silence, the trucks and machines are abandoned. All movement frozen.

"I may not even be pregnant," I say softly.

"Yeah, that's true, but if you are, this would fix it. I'll pay for it. It can be between you and me," he adds.

"I'll think about it," I say.

"Okay, let me know as soon as you know anything," he demands.

"I will," I say turning away.

"Oh, and Julie, don't tell Scott anything about this conversation," he reminds me.

"I won't," I agree.

I'm afraid to tell Scott. His father may never let us see each other then. I'm afraid of his father. Crossing Maple I look back at the building site that is encased by strong fencing, protecting its construction.

Several blocks later I pass through the stone wall entrance to Prospect Park and walk two short blocks. Turning the corner, I see several fire trucks in front of my house. There are cars parked all over the street and people, so many people. A loud ringing fills my ears, the street narrows, and I follow it to the destruction. But my legs are weak, and I don't know if I'll make it all the way. I don't want to see it, but I do. I have to see it. And now I see my life up in smoke, piles of ashes. The flames burned my hope. My dreams are just charred memories. But was hope already gone? Were my dreams snuffed out before the heat could melt them? My life, my hope, my dreams, taken away, not by flames, not by heat or smoke; by me.

CHAPTER THREE

THE NIGHT OF THE FIRE, my family stays with my nana. My sister and I kneel next to Nana's bed and pray. A large picture of Jesus and the Sacred Heart hangs above our heads. I have a lot to pray for tonight. I begin by praying for our cat who died in the fire today. Nana reminds me to be thankful for my blessings, but none come to mind. When we are finished, we make the sign of the cross, and I lie down on the cot that's been pushed up to the wall, as my sister gets into Nana's bed. I feel a splash of holy water as I pull the sheets up. Nana throws holy water at every opportunity. This time it feels appropriate. I can hear my sister crying, and I tell her it will be okay. I'm not really sure though. I don't know what tomorrow will be like. I don't know where we will live or what we will wear, but I tell her again that everything is going to be fine, and then sleep takes over.

We've been at Nana's for less than a day, but it feels like forever.

"Good news," my mother says, walking into the kitchen.

Everyone is seated around the Formica table, except my father who is at our house trying to salvage what he can.

"We can move into the Rosens' house," she continues.

The Rosens live across the street from us and have been in Israel for close to a year.

"Go through these boxes of clothes and see if you can use anything. All the neighbors collected them for us," she says putting them down on the table.

I haven't seen my mother cry once throughout this ordeal. My father is crying all the time. I guess she has to be strong for him and for us. Yesterday was my twin brothers' birthday. The day of the fire. My mother doesn't want to forget their birthday, so she has a cake and ice cream for later, and we'll sing happy birthday. They'll have to wait for their special dinner, though. My mother makes us anything we want on our birthdays. My favorite is duck with orange sauce. She lights candles and we use the good china and eat in the dining room. My sister usually asks for roast beef and Yorkshire pudding. My brothers have simpler taste, spaghetti and meatballs. Next year, maybe next year we can have their special birthday dinner.

My father comes back from working on the house all day. His hair, face, clothes, all covered in soot with a burnt smell that permeates whatever it comes in contact with. He looks exhausted and depleted. He heads upstairs to clean up. Nana has made her famous chicken and rice soup for dinner. Something familiar that comforts.

After dinner, my mother gets the candles out for the cake. When it's ready, we turn the lights off and finally sing happy birthday. It's chocolate cake, my favorite. We all get a piece and sit around listening to my father talk about the house. I drop my fork on the table and walk, then run to the bathroom and throw up. I'm sure I'm just upset with everything that's happened. I realize that I haven't checked all day. I'm sure I'll get it any time now.

I know the house across the street really well. I've helped Mrs. Rosen with her Passover dinners. I'd serve different parts of the meal according to the bible verses as Dr. Rosen read them. Then clean the kitchen while everyone was eating. I managed to kill all their plants one winter while they were in Israel, but they forgave me. I'm sharing a room with my sister here. We've pulled a daybed out and keep it that way all the time, so there is not a lot of room. I went to the drug store today to buy a box of tampons and put them under the sink in the main bathroom. They are there for when I get my period.

I have to get ready because I'm going out with my girlfriends for my birthday tonight, first to the movies and then to the bars in New Rochelle, with fake I.D. We all walked to an office building in North White Plains after school one day and paid a little old man ten dollars for a laminated card that says we are students at the College of White Plains and eighteen years old.

At the end of the night we go to the Eastchester diner where we only get the cheesecake. That's why we come. That's why everyone comes. I'm not eating as much as I used to. I just take a bite of Melissa's.

"It's because of the fire and moving. I don't know, I've just lost my appetite," I tell Debbie on the way to the bathroom. But once there I ask her if she will come with me tomorrow. Come with me to Planned Parenthood. She doesn't ask me any questions; she knows I don't want to talk about it now. We'll talk on the way there. Tomorrow.

The room is feeling smaller and smaller, grayer and grayer as I watch the doctor's lips move. I can't hear him. I can't hear what he is saying. When he leaves, I slide off the table, my feet searching for the floor. I stumble to the door that is heavy and nearly impossible to open. I have to get to Debbie. She's in the waiting room. But the hallway grows longer and longer with each step. I have to get to Debbie, to the way it was, the way it is supposed to be. Finally I reach the waiting room, see Debbie, and motion to her. She follows me to the doorway, out the lobby and onto the sidewalk.

"Julie, are you okay?" she asks.

And the words that I couldn't hear pass through my lips, "I'm pregnant."

And now it's true.

———————

Sitting on the edge of my parents' bed, I stare at the closed door to the bathroom, then crawl over and look into the keyhole. There is my mother. She looks different through the keyhole. Will she still love me, if I tell her through the keyhole? Will she still be my mom, if I tell her through the keyhole? What will I unlock, if I tell her through the keyhole? Will her love and acceptance come spilling out or will it be her anger and shame?

I turn the key slowly, "Mom?"

"What is it?"

I back away onto the bed then back to the keyhole once more, slowly turning.

"Mom I have to tell you something."

"What is it?"

"I can't tell you."

"Tell me what?"

The key turning, "I can't say."

"Oh God, you're not pregnant!"

I drop the key.

"Hmmm hmmm."

"Oh Julie, oh my God I can't believe it. I can't even talk to you right now. I'm too upset. Oh my God, oh God."

"I'm sorry Mom. I'm really so sorry."

It's been a few endless days since I told my mother. I stay out of the way and spend most of my time lying in the day bed my sister and I share. I can look down the hallway from here. Today is the first time I've spotted my father since the news broke. He walks into the kitchen and looks but gives me no expression. Scott's stepfather is here. I'm just going to stay right here in bed until or unless I'm called. I sleep all the time now. My body is changing. I'm getting rounder in my stomach. I feel full. My clothes are getting tight. I don't think I should ask for new clothes. I can hear them all in the kitchen. They are talking about me. They are talking about adoption. They will only consider adoption. They will not consider abortion. Marriage is out. Adoption, that's it. I unzip my pants part way. There, now I can breathe. At least I don't feel sick right now. I feel sick every morning and then I throw up. I'm going to close my eyes until or unless they call me.

CHAPTER FOUR

I NEVER TIRE OF HEARING my mother tell the story. Her words never change, yet it always sounds new. "Your father and I were walking out the door to go shopping when the phone rang. It was Election Day and we both had the day off. Dad didn't want me to answer it, but somehow I thought it was important. And it was. It was our caseworker with the news that we had a baby girl. We were so excited and forgot what we were supposed to do that day. We spent the entire day shopping for you to get everything ready so we could pick you up the next day."

When I was younger, I wondered what would have happened if they decided not to answer the phone. Would the caseworker have given me to the next parents on the list? Now that I'm seventeen, I think there was less chance involved. I was five months old on that Election Day. On that day I was born to my parents. I was their first-born and the first grandchild on both sides. I was loved and cherished. But, throughout the years, I've thought about my first birthday; my first mother. Was I loved and cherished by her? Did she hold me? Did she feed me? Did she want me? I can see her with her dark hair; her soft voice whispering to me as she gently rocks me. Then I see her crying knowing that she has to let me go so I can be with my family. The family who has been waiting for me. I'm crying too, because I know her smell, her voice, her touch. After that Election Day, I would come to learn a new smell, a new voice, a new touch and I wouldn't want to let that mother go either, the one I would call Mom.

My daddy gives me a ride on his shoe. I have to hold on tight because he swings his leg and then he whisks me up in his arms and plops me on top of the refrigerator and catches me as I jump. Daddy always gives me a piggyback ride up to my bed that is cozy with a fluffy blanket dotted with tiny lavender flowers. My soft animals, Lambie and Kitty, sit on top of my pillow waiting for me to tuck them in next to me. Daddy has to make sure the leprechaun isn't hiding, then we say our prayers. I know every word of "Now I Lay Me Down to Sleep." I listen carefully as Daddy says the "Our Father" and "Hail Mary." I'm still learning those. When we finish, he asks me if I know what it means to be adopted, and I always say, "it means you love me." "That's right," he tells me, smiling. Then Daddy gives me a great big hug and a kiss. I ask him for a glass of water and when he comes back he gives me another kiss. He leaves the door open just a little, so a slice of light sits on the floor, signaling that he's never far away. I love my daddy.

————

On a dark, chilly November morning in 1961, my mother woke me up early. She pulled the freshly ironed pale blue dress with delicate smocking on the front over my head and perfectly tied the bow in the back. She found the special hook to button my Mary Janes and helped me put on my blue coat with velvet trim and the matching hat. My father warmed the car, and I hopped in the back seat as my excitement built. Then we began our drive to pick up my new baby twin brothers at the New York Foundling Hospital.

The waiting room was painted in standard green hospital paint, with beige leather couches and a few odd chairs that quickly began to fill up. I wasn't sure if everyone was there to pick up their babies too. A lady dressed in a long black dress and a black bonnet walked toward us smiling as she held a baby in each arm.

Jumping up my father said, "Oh, Sister, let me help you."

He took one of the babies from her and she handed the other to my mother. My father propped the baby next to me as he knelt in front of the couch. I patted my new baby brother's leg and introduced myself. My parents couldn't get over how big and healthy the babies were. We had already picked out names. One baby was Christopher and the other Stephen. We just had to remember who was who.

"Oh they really are identical, it's hard to tell them apart," my mother said.

But I could tell them apart from that very first moment.

The babies began to fuss, catching the attention of Sister who picked them up and started to carry them out of the room toward the endless hallway.

"Bring back my babies, those are my babies," I yelled, running after her.

"I'll bring them back," she said turning her head back toward me.

But I didn't believe her. Could babies be taken away that easily?

My mother is brushing my hair when the phone rings, then squeezes my cheeks before answering it. I hate when she does that, but she says it gives me rosy cheeks. As I run through the kitchen to go play outside, I hear her say, "they aren't lying, they are adopted." Patti is waiting for me at the door. She is my very best friend in the world. Today we are going to ride our bikes. Patti's sister, Peggy, just taught me how to ride a two-wheeler. She held the back of the seat and ran with me, over and over and over, until I could do it myself. Now I'm ready to ride down the back road with the bigger kids. Soon I'll be able to ride my bike on the hills at each end of the road. One hill is called "Monaghan's Hill" and the other is called "John - John's Hill." You can have a hill named after you if you live next to it.

Patti and I have been riding all afternoon and stop at my house for cookies and milk. Patti loves to dunk her cookies, but I like mine crisp. When we finish, we go outside to ride just a little more. Later when my father comes home, my mother tells him that a lady who lives on the road behind us called and said that the twins were handing out money, but worse than that they were lying and telling the other children that they were adopted. Once again I heard my mother say, "they aren't lying they are adopted." I'm not sure what all this means. I don't know yet why our neighbor is more upset that my brothers are adopted than she is that they were handing out all that money. I can't figure it out yet. Maybe someday I will.

———

Patti and I stop and call for Tommy Alexander on the way to the forest. We have our lunches and a blanket with us. Our moms said we could have a picnic in the forest. Our block is about twenty houses long, where the front yards are on a busy street, but the driveways empty into a quiet back road. We like to yell, "slow down, private road," at any car that looks like it doesn't belong. That's what the grownups do. While we wait for Tommy to come outside, we circle the lucky tree that grows right through his porch. Tommy circles it once and then we race down the driveway. We reach the forest at the end of the block, blanketed with pine needles that have fallen from the giant evergreens. As we enter the forest, we can see that we have been taken from our castle while we slept after drinking the potion that was prepared by the stable hand, who was really an evil villain. We must find the King's horses and charge the castle to reclaim the Kingdom.

"I wish my brother was here, he could be the evil villain," Patti says.

"I'll turn into the villain later," offers Tommy.

Once the horses are freed and we gallop back to the stable and the villain is poisoned, we are ready to nestle onto the picnic blanket that we have set on the soft pine needles. Patti and I decide that we will collect pinecones after lunch. Tommy agrees, and we open up our lunches and start to eat. This is the most magical picnic we've ever had. Sunrays flow through the branches, creating shadows that surround the blanket, and occasionally a wind rustles through the trees, whispering "who?" I don't understand. Maybe someday I will know who.

———————

It's been almost four years since we sat in that waiting room at the New York Foundling Hospital. My parents, the twins and I ride the elevator up to the third floor of the Department of Social Services. We are here to pick up our new baby sister. We pile into a small office and my mother sits in a wooden chair at the edge of the desk. A few people come into the room and one of the ladies is holding our baby in a white blanket. She hands her to my mother.

My mother looking into her eyes, says, "she's so beautiful. I can't believe how beautiful. Look at her eyes. She's just so beautiful."

My father looks over my mother's shoulder, and I can see how happy he is. My brothers and I think she looks like any other baby. But when the lady asks what I think about my new sister, I tell her that I think she is beautiful, and I mention how happy I am to have a sister. We haven't decided on a name yet. Now that I am seven, my suggestions are taken more seriously. My friend's name is Diane. She has tons of Barbie's and I love being at her house. My mother likes the name Diane and suggests that we change the spelling and add another "n". Then she would be named Dianne for my Grandmother, Anne. So before taking our new baby home, we all agree to show her off to my grandmother, who works at an all-boys Catholic high school, not far from our house. We stop to pick up ice cream to bring with us as we surprise her with a new granddaughter and a new namesake. My grandmother is the school's switchboard operator, so she sits in the main hall. I'm not sure she knows what to make of us, as she sees us coming through the front door.

"Meet your granddaughter," my mother says.

My grandmother loves babies as much as my mother and rushes over to scoop her from my mother's arms. I'm sure I see tears in my grandmother's eyes, but she's hiding them with her smile.

We go outside and sit at the picnic benches at the edge of the school's duck pond. The ice cream tastes especially sweet.

"We have the perfect family now; two and two. The girls are our bookends," my father says.

My brothers throw bits of their cones to the ducks, while my grandmother feeds my sister some ice cream. I watch as she puts just a dab of the sweet cream on her tongue, as my mother begins to protest.

"See she loves it," interrupts my grandmother.

Then my baby sister's legs and arms wiggle as she fixes her big green eyes on the cup asking for more. She is the sweetest baby in the world and makes everyone so happy. I want my family to stay just as we are on this beautiful August afternoon.

My sister has been home for two days, and today we are bringing her to the pool. Whenever we go to the pool it's after lunch. There is a one hour rule between eating and swimming. By then the water has been warmed by the direct afternoon sun. My brothers have to stay in the shallow end, but I'm learning how to swim, so I'll venture out to the deep end. Along with our towels and kickboards, we have baby stuff: a carriage, diaper bag, umbrella, extra clothes and a special cooler for bottles. My mother finds a shady spot near the corner and we put everything by her chair on the grass, and then rush to the pool after she gives us the okay. Soon I am a mermaid exploring the sea floor. When I come up for air, I wave to my mother and she waves back.

My brother, Chris, yells, "Mommy, watch this."

He's learning to swim under water.

He swims to the stairs and asks, "How was that?"

She claps and says, "that was terrific!"

We have so much fun here. I wish my mother could come in the water, but she has to feed the baby. When we are wrinkly and our eyes are stinging, we get out, shivering and beg for frozen Milky Ways. We each put a hand on the carriage and help wheel toward the snack bar.

One of the other mothers stops us and asks, "whose baby is that?"

"Ours," my mother answers as my brothers and I smile proudly.

"I didn't know you had a baby," she says.

"We just adopted her," my mother says smiling at our baby.

"Oh," the lady begins.

I notice her smile goes away and so does my mother's and suddenly I know that being adopted is different, maybe it's not a good thing. I don't understand so I ask my mother with my eyes, but she doesn't answer me. She looks away and continues pushing the carriage toward the snack bar, but I know from her silence that we can't talk about adoption. We should probably keep it a secret.

———————

Our house with the back road is feeling smaller and smaller. That's what my mother thinks. I love my house and my block. I hate to think about leaving.

"I don't want to move. I don't want to leave Patti," I plead.

"She can come and stay overnight," my mother assures me.

The Collins' Brothers moving truck pulls up to our house on a hot July morning. Patti and I each pull out a few strands of our hair and exchange them, swearing we'll keep them forever. Our new house is so big that we each can have our own room. We have so many parties in our new house. But I don't have much fun, because I see my father getting drunk more and more. I used to only see him drunk at Nana's house, where we go most Sundays for dinner and my mother tells him to behave himself. That's what she says when she doesn't want him to get drunk. Now he hardly ever behaves himself. There is a built in cabinet in the family room, where he keeps the liquor. When he gets home from work he goes directly to the cabinet and unlocks it with the old fashioned key kept way up high on the top. He brings the bottles into the pink tiled kitchen that my mother hates and will be painted soon. He pours scotch for my mother first and then a whiskey sour for himself. We don't eat dinner together in our new house. My mother says that she and my father like to eat later. So my brothers, sister and I eat in the dinette, while my parents have cocktails at the kitchen counter. My mother usually has two, sometimes three. My father doesn't stop until he falls asleep in his big chair, but when he doesn't he becomes mean. Sometimes he hits me with the belt. I don't know why, I guess I should be better. Maybe I did something during the day. I always say "Daddy no, no Daddy, I'm sorry," but he doesn't hear me. I don't think my mother can hear me either. When he doesn't behave, he and my mother yell at each other, but the next morning everything is always fine and the red marks on my skin are almost gone. Our big house is really noisy. I miss my small house. It was quieter, and I must have been better there.

Since my father hung a tire swing up, our yard has become a popular place to play. A few girls from my neighborhood are lining up to take turns. The rest of us are riding bikes skillfully around the curving walkways, as though we're on a high wire. We zigzag, lap after lap, peddle quickly and only slow down for the sharp turns. My friend, Robin, from across the street stops riding to have a turn on the swing. I drop my bike and follow. The line is getting longer as more and more kids hear about our swing.

While waiting for her turn, Sharon who lives next door and has only recently become my friend, asks, "Do you know your real mother?" Startled I don't know what to say, but I know what she's asking. She wonders where I came from and who I am, who I really am. I don't know, it's complicated, I can't know, those are the rules.

"No," I finally answer.

"You know she's adopted," Sharon announces to the others as they look at me. I feel my face become as red as my bike.

"I have to go in now. I have to do something this afternoon. Maybe I can play when I get back," I say picking up my bike and riding it to the back stairs. Once inside the mudroom, I am relieved to have made it just in time so they didn't see my tears. I try not to let people know that it hurts to be different. That it feels shameful to be different. I especially don't want to let my parents know. They would be really hurt if they knew I felt different. I know this from their silence.

It's just after lunch and we are settling back into our desks. The girls spent recess jumping rope. We are just learning Double-Dutch. The boys played basketball with Father. Sr. Margaret tells us to quiet down. She has just begun wearing the new habit. It comes just below her knee and her head is just partially covered so her dark hair frames her face. Sister seems light and free now, no longer held down by heavy fabric and pinch tight cardboard around her face. She asks us to take out our science books and turn to chapter eight, "Genetics."

"There is a project for this unit, so I'd like you to bring in pictures of your parents and of yourselves. We can study the similarities between parents and their children," she says.

The class is intently listening as she points to the back bulletin board that she set up while we were at recess.

"There is a section on the left for pictures of parents and pictures of their children go on the right," she explains.

"I'd like to make this fun, so I will mix everyone up and you will have to try and match who belongs to whom," she continues.

Of course anything that resembles fun is always well received, so cheers erupt around the room. But I know that this will only highlight that I don't belong. Didn't Sister remember that I'm adopted? Did she think about me? My stomach begins to feel funny and continues through the afternoon. At the end of the day, while everyone is packing up and the buses are being called, I approach her desk, not really knowing what to say.

"Sister, um, the pictures that you want us to bring in. Um well you know I'm adopted, and," I begin.

"Yes, I was going to tell you that you can still play the game, you can take guesses of whose parents are whose," she tells me.

"Okay," I say forcing a smile.

But I really feel angry and hate her for this. She thinks that I want to play this stupid game on the wall. I wanted her to tell me that she had forgotten that I was adopted and that she would never do anything to embarrass me or make me feel shame for not being good enough to be on that wall. But I'm not good enough. I have to watch from the outside. I can see that now. It's right in front of me. I have parents, but we have no similarities. We couldn't be matched up on a board, even if I pretended or kept it a secret or changed the subject. I still couldn't play.

CHAPTER FIVE

THE FIRST PHONE CALL my mother makes after learning of my pregnancy is to our parish priest. They have a meeting this evening, and a solemn mood hovers across the house, as I'm left to finish dinner with my brothers and sister and clean the kitchen.

"Ready?" my father asks.

"I guess," my mother answers.

Burdened, they slowly move down the few steps to the front door. The gravity of the situation is magnified as the door opens and our burnt house looms within sight. Soot cascades from the boarded windows and piles of debris line the yard. There is a smell that lingers and will not allow us to forget for more than a short time. My brothers and sister don't know about me yet, so they think my parents are going to a meeting with the insurance man. I know the truth, and I can't imagine what is in store for me when they get back. As I wash the counters and load the dishwasher, I try to imagine them sitting in Father Gannon's office discussing my future. When they return, I'm waiting in the living room.

I'm afraid to ask, but I do anyway. "What did Father say?"

"He thinks we should send you away. He said you are the one who got yourself into this, and it would be easier for everyone," my mother says.

My father walks into the kitchen and begins to pour a drink.

"He suggested a place across the river," she continues.

I look at her for a while, but I can't tell how she feels.

"I didn't like that idea," she finally says. "It sounded much too harsh. We will just have to find a way to keep you out of sight for the next several months. Your grandparents can't know, our friends can't know, and of course you won't be able to go back to Good Counsel."

I nod my head in agreement.

The next morning, as I sit in front of a bowl of Cheerios, my mother is on the phone with my school.

"I'm very disappointed too, but with the fire, we just can't afford to send Julie back in September."

When she hangs up the phone, we both have the sense of one more loss, another dream dashed. I won't graduate from Good Counsel, something my parents always wanted for me.

Week after week my belly is growing bigger and bigger. I'm growing everywhere else too. My face is fuller and my breasts sit on top of a ledge that is my stomach. My thighs rub against each other and my feet are swollen. When I feel my baby fluttering, I'm overwhelmed by love. Some days I picture a baby boy with blonde hair and Scott's eyes. Other days I'm sure I have a baby girl growing inside of me. Every night I open the drawer of my white and gold night table and pull out the one book I have on pregnancy. It describes how my baby is growing and what changes are occurring. I've read it cover to cover several times, but I'm still not tired of it. I push on my stomach and I feel a strong kick, we play this game, my baby and me. I dream that I can be pregnant forever and then no one can have my baby, just me. My mother has never been pregnant so I don't have anyone to talk to about what's happening to my body. I don't recognize the lines that have appeared all over my stomach and thighs, my neck is a different color than the rest of me. My friends don't know what to make of me either. Just a few months ago we were hanging out at Nicky's having a slice, and now I get heartburn when I eat pizza. I try to limit sightings of me by not crossing the invisible perimeter of the twenty block radius of downtown that I have drawn. These days I look less and less like a giggly teenager and more and more like a caged polar bear. I have traded my landlubber jeans and cute tops for my big white bathrobe. My back hurts unless I sit straight up with the arm of the couch supporting me. That's how I sit when I watch "All in the Family." Gloria Stivic and I are going through our pregnancies together, but she's married to Michael Stivic and Archie and Edith are really excited.

———

My mother calls the public high school and sets me up with a tutor, so I can continue earning credits and graduate in June. I meet with my tutor every morning for a few hours in the basement of the Ridgeview Congregational Church. The cement walls have been painted a pale yellow and bright floral curtains added. But all of this makes the linoleum floor look quite faded and there is no disguising the dampness. Worn and rusty folding chairs that require me to sit close to the edge surround long metal tables. My tutor is a tiny lady with a very short pixie haircut. She reminds me of Tinkerbell, if Tinkerbell wore khakis with crewneck sweaters and was brilliant. My tutor sips coffee out of a rainbow mug that she brings each morning from home, as we both begin to browse the New York Times.

She quickly calls my attention to particular articles. This is my first experience with public education, and even though Jesus is just one floor up, I can't help notice that he is never mentioned. I have been introduced to the idea of discussing issues and not worrying about offending God or inadvertently inciting "An Occasion to Sin." With my tutor, my opinions matter and seem valid. I have not overlooked the fact that this is a blessing within my life's turmoil.

"Have you ever watched Nova on Channel 13?" my brilliant tutor inquires.

"No, but I have heard of it," I answer, wishing I were a bit more intellectually gifted.

"Well I'd like you to watch it Sunday night. They are repeating 'The Lost World of the Maya' and we can discuss it next week."

I have never been so eager to watch something on PBS, as I am right at this moment. She describes the Mayan Civilization with vivid details and a dramatic flair, and suddenly I am considering becoming an anthropologist. My tutor is opening my world up, and I'm feeling quite hopeful in this basement. At the end of the morning, she puts her books in the canvas bag she always carries, and I gather up my books and carry them in front of my belly as we walk up the steps to the street.

"Would you like a ride?" my tutor offers.

"Oh, no thank you, I'm fine," I say, knowing I will probably regret not accepting her kind offer after a few blocks.

———

We are back in our house now, which is really not our house but a construction site. We have a Coleman stove on the porch, a sink downstairs and a toilet up. The tub on the third floor was spared. We use piles of sheet rock as tables and chairs. My mother asks us to think of it as a camping trip, but it's neither fun nor adventurous. I try to hide from the construction workers, who have descended upon us, by staying in my room as much as possible, but I do have to appear from time to time. One of the carpenters talks to me. I think he is the youngest worker here, maybe just a year or two older than me. The other day he told me that he thought I was brave. I like having someone to talk to, someone I don't have to hide from, but it's hard for me to make a friend right now. I'm not sure who I am. I don't recognize me. I don't recognize anything. There is construction everywhere; throughout the house, throughout my body.

———

Every Sunday, my mother and I go to the 11:15 Mass. My mother parks at the end of St. Bernard's parking lot and squeezes our station wagon between two others. As we walk, I try to button my mother's green corduroy coat with the fur collar that is temporarily mine, but it barely buttons anymore. This is the only coat that sort of fits me, and I know it will be my only winter coat until the baby is born. My mother and I have been attending the Spanish Mass ever since I began showing. My mother says she loves the music and the celebratory praising, but I know why we really go to the 11:15. We sit close to the back on the right side every week. They give communion in the rear of the church too, so I don't have to go up to the altar. After a few months, I have learned when to stand, sit and kneel, although I can't really kneel anymore. I try, but I end up leaning back. I know a few words to some of the hymns and distract myself by reading the missal and trying to figure out the Gospel in Spanish. When Mass is over, we wait for the priest to leave, genuflect and quickly exit through the side door. I'm not sure even Jesus sees me there.

I've been alternating between two maternity tops. I have two pair of maternity jeans that may split in the rear if I'm not careful, so my mother and I are going shopping at a maternity store on Mamaroneck Avenue. My mother finds a spot and parallel parks a few stores down, while I look for change to feed the meter. The stores on Mamaroneck Avenue are not very large. This store is no exception with the inventory tightly arranged, so I feel especially awkward as my belly stops me at every turn. My mother and I are experienced shoppers and quickly separate and whisk the hangers right to left, eliminating most pieces and every now and then pulling out possibilities.

Fully immersed in our tasks, we look up as a woman approaches and says, "I thought that was you. I almost didn't recognize you outside of your store."

It must be one of her customers. My mother works at a store in Hartsdale, the next town over, where she is an expert in fabric cutting, knitting, pattern selection and anything else that has to do with sewing.

"Who are you shopping for?" the woman continues.

"Oh, I'm here with my daughter," my mother says, realizing she's been caught.

"Oh my, she looks so young," the woman says.

"She does, she's nineteen. She got married very young," my mother lies.

"Well, congratulations."

"Thank you," my mother says.

"I have to run. Nice seeing you," the woman finally says.

And we are left to endure the tension. I'm sure my mother is already thinking of what she is going to say and is sick about the possibility of the people she works with finding out. Maybe she'll have to make up another lie to cover this one. That's usually how it goes. I hold up a dark paisley top for her approval.

"Oh, that's pretty," she says.

"Yeah I like it too," I add.

I spend each Wednesday afternoon with the social worker at the Westchester Adoption Agency. I'm happy to see the stately brick colonial house as I turn the corner. It's getting more and more uncomfortable for me to walk across town these days. I'm right on time as I open the freshly painted door and begin up the staircase that wraps around the center hall. The waiting room is filled with toys and pale pink and blue wallpaper. Before I can sit down, I'm escorted by the receptionist into an empty office.

"We are expecting adoptive parents for an appointment shortly," the receptionist says, "and we'd prefer you not to be here when they arrive."

Eventually my social worker finds me and brings me to her office. She sits behind the desk, and I sit at one of the two chairs facing her. She looks washed out with her gray hair and beige cardigan with a white peter pan collar. There is a large window behind her, and I can see the starkness of the branches. The sun has changed since last week, when I couldn't look at her without being blinded. I've been coming here since the end of summer, when the leaves were green and lush, and I've watched them slowly change and then disappear.

"So, how has your week been? How are you feeling?" my social worker inquires.

"I'm feeling pretty well," I respond.

"Have you given thought to what we were talking about last week?" she asks.

"You mean how can Scott and I take care of the baby?" I answer as she nods. "I know that I can take care of a baby. I've taken care of babies my whole life. Scott just has to find a job, so we can live in an apartment."

"Have you thought about how much an apartment costs, how would you finish school, and what kind of job could Scott get?" she demands.

"Umm, I was thinking that maybe Scott could get a job with his father in construction and we wouldn't need a big apartment. I don't know yet how I would finish school, but I can check," I say.

"How can you finish school and take care of a baby. What if Scott doesn't get a job?" she asks.

"Well, maybe the baby could go to a foster mother for just a little while. You know, just until we can get things ready?" I try.

"No. That's not possible," my social worker says.

"But, I want to keep my baby. I know I will be a good mother. I love my baby, and I don't think anybody can love my baby as much as I do," I say, choking back tears.

I look away from her and turn my head toward the corner of the room. As the silence lingers, I feel my baby moving.

"We can talk more about this next week," she says loudly, enough to startle me.

Holding on to the arms of the chair, I lift myself up, take my coat from the other chair and put it on as I walk out the doorway. I know I can push the tears back until I get down the stairs and out the front door.

The clinic is attached to the hospital, where I go for my monthly exam and get a prescription for vitamins. I have less than three months until my due date, so today I was given instructions for the hospitalization and costs, along with insurance forms. I put them on the counter with the mail in the kitchen when I got home. I know my parents always check the mail, and it won't go unnoticed. The rest of the kitchen is usually cluttered with piles of paper. I'm the first to get home from school each day, and I spend my time cleaning. I love to see the kitchen and family room tidy, if only for that short period of time. Our new kitchen is beautiful and opens to the family room, with the fireplace that I cleaned out the other day. Little by little our house is transforming back into a home. But once everyone begins to straggle in, I retreat to my room.

That night before dinner, I ask my mother if she saw the paperwork. She did.

"It occurred to me that someone in Dad's office might see the insurance forms if he submits them. That would be just awful. I'm not sure what we are going to do," she says.

I take my seat at the table and wonder what I should say or do. I go to the clinic, because it's free, but I guess the hospital isn't. I know my parents were not happy when they found out the adoption agency didn't pay any medical costs, especially my mother. This is just one more problem that I've caused and can't fix. And a week later, the insurance forms are right where I left them. I've picked them up several times as I neaten the pile.

A couple of months before I'm due to have the baby I drive to Scott's new school. He is officially out of White Plains and under the watchful eye of his father. He went there after a brief yet significant criminal activity. I first learned about it just before we moved back into our house, when my mother handed me the newspaper. As I scanned the front page, my eyes spotted a story about three people arrested for breaking, entering and stealing equipment from the high school.

Scott called me last night and asked if I would come up. I haven't spoken to him in a couple of months. Melissa drove me up one day, but his father wouldn't let us in. As I get off the Taconic Parkway, I follow the directions Scott gave me from the exit. I find his school and as I drive to the front of the building, see him and wave. He smiles as he walks toward the car and opens the door.

"Hey, thanks for coming up," he says staring at my belly that's just shy of scraping the steering wheel.

"It's fine, I wasn't doing anything this afternoon," I reply, knowing that I don't do anything any afternoon.

"Where should we go?" I ask as I drive out of the parking lot.

"I don't know. We can drive around a little," he answers.

There is an awkwardness that is new between us. He tells me that he'd like to take a drive down to White Plains.

"Okay," I answer, realizing that he probably just needed a ride to buy drugs.

On the way down the parkway, Scott remembers a place where we can take a walk. I pull into the deserted park, dismissing the idea that he is using me as transportation. We find a wide path that is covered by brown leaves, evidence of autumn's near departure. We walk along the exposed brush, through the cold damp air, while the sky darkens. I'm trying to keep up with Scott when he stops and waits, then leans down and kisses me on the cheek, the kind an old friend gives when saying goodbye.

"We better get back," he suggests.

So I turn and follow. Rain is falling lightly by the time we reach the car. My tires are not very good, so I drive slowly down the parkway. I ask him what he wants to do in White Plains and it's clear that his plans don't include me. I glance at him just as he is doing the same, and I can see that he's not looking at me the way he used to. I don't think he knows what he ever saw in me. He looks angry. I'm sure he's embarrassed by me. The sound of the windshield wipers is exaggerated by the silence between us. I get off the exit and drive downtown.

"You can just drop me off at this next corner," he tells me in a voice I'm not familiar with. "Hey, thanks a lot. I really appreciate it," he says as he shuts the door.

Foolish. Stupid. I sit watching him cross the street. And now I know what I probably always knew: that in the end he'd shut the door on me, shut the door on raising our baby, and shut the door on the dream of our being a family.

One evening after dinner, my father tells me Mr. Caven handles private adoptions. They went out with the Cavens for dinner over the weekend. They have been friends for years, and I guess they sought some legal advice between cocktails and courses. My mother adds the news that they cover all medical expenses and anything I may need.

"That means you can go to a private doctor and we can get you more clothes," she says with a look of relief.

But I feel really uneasy about the entire turn of events.

"I don't think that a private adoption will be right for my baby. I know that the agency does really stringent home studies," I say.

"They do home studies too. Mr. Caven mentioned that," my mother replies.

"Why don't they just go through a regular adoption agency?" I ask. "There must be something wrong with people if they can't go through an agency. I just don't want to use him," I insist.

"You are going to use him, goddammit," my father says, slamming down his drink.

"I want to stay with the adoption agency. Please," I say.

"They won't pay for anything, and we don't have that kind of money," my mother says.

I knew my mother would bring up money. She always brings up money when they're drinking and that makes my father angrier. She's constantly reminding him about how he messed up with the house insurance and left us forty thousand dollars underinsured. I think she brings it up every week.

"I don't want to switch now," I plead with a growing sense of doom and desperation.

"You will do it. That's it," my father roars.

I can't back down. Private adoption is for people who can't adopt for some reason. It's about money. This is my baby I'm protecting.

"No. I won't," I barely get out as I feel my father's hand rip across my face.

"It's her baby!" yells, my brother, Chris.

He stands between my father and me as my mother disappears.

"It's her baby, let her do what she wants," he screams.

And, as expected, he is now the recipient of my father's rage. As I hold my stomach, I try to push them away from each other. I shout at my father to stop, but he doesn't. Defeated I go up to my room escaping the frenzy of fists. I can hear Chris's bravery and hate myself for not protecting him. I hate myself for not protecting my baby. I know I'll just do as they say. I hate myself for always doing what they say, but in the end I always do.

———

"Come in Julie," my social worker says at our regular Wednesday afternoon meeting. I take my usual seat, and she closes the door and walks behind the desk.

"So, how are you feeling today? You have gotten so much bigger just in this last week," she notices.

"I'm a little more uncomfortable, but I'm okay," I lie.

I'm a lot more uncomfortable, I'm having a hard time breathing, and my back hurts no matter how I sit.

"So how was your week?" she asks.

"Well, my parents have decided that I have to use their lawyer, and we will do a private adoption," I say, and instantly see that I have said something that has changed everything.

"Private adoptions are not handled as carefully and do not have the same standards as a traditional agency. Are you aware of that? Are they aware of that?" she asks.

"I know that they will do a home study and they pay all the expenses," I say suddenly defending this decision.

"I know that it is unfortunate that we can't help you with the medical expenses, but that is against our policies, and we think it would not be ethical," she says sternly.

"I tried to talk them out of it," I say wanting her to know this wasn't my idea.

"The home study they do will certainly not be as in depth as ours," she continues.

I know she is right and I know it's already been decided. I try to look at her, but I think she is angered by all of this.

"Can I still come and see you Wednesday afternoons?" I ask softly.

"I'm sorry but if you don't use our agency for placement, we can no longer provide you services," she explains. And then I understand what this was all about. She just wanted my baby.

"Oh, okay," I say trying not to reveal how betrayed I feel.

I thought she cared about me. She doesn't know me. She doesn't know that underneath I am really a good girl. I wish she knew that. I have to leave and never come back.

———— —— ——

Our house never feels warm enough, especially on a day like today. The gray sky and stinging air suggest snow's momentary arrival. The taped and spackled walls are illuminated by the roaring fire that my father lit. The dogs huddle in front of the fireplace, while I sit on the couch wrapped in a blue afghan that my Aunt Nora knitted years ago and by some fluke survived the fire. If only I had a book to read and our meeting could be canceled, it would be a perfect day. But Mr. Caven, the lawyer, is coming over this afternoon, so I can choose the adoptive parents. My normally labored breathing is exacerbated by this knowledge, and the baby has been particularly active all day. I'm sure this is no coincidence. My baby must know what I am doing. I don't want to do this. I hate myself for doing this. I hate my parents for forcing me to do this. I hate Scott for leaving me with no option. I'm worn out, and I'm finally worn down. I can hear their voices, all of them. The ones that have told me that if I love my baby I will do what is best for the baby. I'd just be selfish if I kept my baby. What kind of life could I give a baby; no way to support the baby, no father for the baby, no help from my family. The only thing I have to give my baby is hope. Maybe the family I choose can give my baby a good life. Maybe they will love my baby too.

When Mr. Caven arrives, we all take our places. My parents sit on the folding chairs by the small round table that separates the kitchen from the family room and Mr. Caven sits next to me on the couch. My brothers and sister are nowhere to be seen given the magnitude of this visit. We exchange niceties and Mr. Caven reaches over and pats my belly.

"It's funny to think that the baby we are talking about is sitting right here," he says with a broad smile.

"Yes, isn't it," my mother replies.

My father clears his throat and nervously taps the table. Mr. Caven leans over and takes out a leather covered legal notepad from his attaché case, as I prop a throw pillow behind me. He opens it slowly, careful not to let my eyes catch any information. He begins by describing a couple who would like to adopt my baby. He talks about their background and how much they want a child.

"How old are they?" I interject.

"Let's see, they are in their forties," he reads.

"In their forties!" I screech looking at my parents and then Mr. Caven who are all in their forties.

"Wow that is really much older than I wanted. What other couples do you have?" I ask.

"Well there is only one other couple," he admits.

"I thought there would be more," I say feeling disappointed.

"This other couple is in their twenties, twenty-seven and twenty-eight. They adopted a baby girl a year ago. Let's see, her name is Jennifer," he reports.

Hearing this, I remember how my mother always told us how unhappy she was being an only child, and I'm encouraged by the idea that my baby will have a sister.

"Why didn't they use a regular agency?" I have to ask.

"Well the wife has diabetes," he says.

"Oh no," I interrupt.

"I know about diabetes. My friend Debbie's mother is a diabetic. Debbie had to save her when she was just a little girl," I continue. "They always have to keep orange juice and jelly in the house and the refrigerator is always filled with insulin vials and hypodermic needles nearby. She just started dialysis a few months ago."

"But this lady has a mild case, nothing like that. It is under control, and she has dark hair like you," he tries to reassure me.

Then I ask about their ethnic background as he looks through the paper work.

"The husband is of German descent and the wife seems to be of Russian descent," he reads.

I don't know anything about Russian or German culture, and I'm not sure it really matters. I'm just trying to be thorough. I'm still not happy about the diabetes, but he would certainly tell me if it were serious. I know Mr. Caven wouldn't do anything to put my baby at risk.

"Oh, the home study," I remind him.

"We have our home studies done by state social workers. It's as detailed as any agency's home study," he says.

I'm feeling slightly better about the home study.

"The baby will have a sister," my mother says brightly.

My father doesn't seem to have an opinion either way.

"They are really a perfect age for a baby," she adds.

And then I tell Mr. Caven about something that I haven't been able to think about. The social worker at the agency told me that I'd have to carry my baby out of the hospital and hand the baby to her as she waits outside of the building. I don't think I can do anything like that I tell him.

"Oh, you won't have to do that!" he says, sounding just as horrified as I was.

"My partner will bring the papers for you to sign on the day of discharge. You won't have to even see the baby if you don't want to," he assures me.

Feeling some vague sense of relief I tell him, "Okay, I guess the younger couple with baby Jennifer would be the best."

"Do you have a picture of them?" I ask.

"No, that is not something we have," he tells me.

"Can they send pictures of the baby so I can make sure everything is all right?" I ask hopefully.

"Oh, I don't think that's a good idea," my mother says.

"We don't do that anyway," Mr. Caven adds.

"You can start going to the regular doctor's office anytime now. And if there is anything else you may need, my office will make the payments," he says.

I close my eyes and begin the process of convincing myself that I've done the right thing. I've chosen the perfect family for my baby. I tell myself over and over the perfect family, the perfect family. I've chosen the perfect family for my baby. If I keep telling myself, then maybe it will be true.

CHAPTER SIX

CHRISTMAS IS GOING ON DOWNSTAIRS. Everything has been decorated. The roast beef is in the oven and the appetizers placed on the trays. I helped set the table earlier, placing the china, silver and glassware in the correct order. We have two trees this year. My brother worked at a tree stand, and brought home an extra tree. The smaller one is in the family room and a large one sits in the living room. I can hear Andy Williams singing "Happy Holidays" as laughter and chatter float up the staircase to my bed where I am stuck with the flu. That is the story, but in truth I am a big balloon covered by my quilt. My two aunts and uncle are here along with my grandmother. My grandfather wasn't up to coming this year, but I'm sure my mother will send enough food home for him to last a month. My Aunt Gloria's laugh is contagious and the laughter gets louder and the voices blend. I know that my grandmother has not seen my Aunt Joan in years, so they have a lot to catch up on. Aunt Joan lives in the city and rarely ventures to the suburbs. I picture my brothers and sister playing board games. I'm missing them all, when I hear the pitter-patter of my four-year-old cousin coming into my room. She doesn't notice how large I've become. She simply dances around my room, which feels festive, a moment of grace and innocence, as I lie here hidden away, having long since lost my innocence. Time passes slowly and I hear my mother's voice and then my grandmother's.

"If she can't come down, then I will go up to her. I'm fine."

Her steps are slow as she journeys up the long staircase. She finally reaches me, out of breath and sits at the edge of my bed and holds my hand.

"It wasn't the same without you," she says, then leans over and gives me a kiss.

"I don't care if I catch what you have," she says, looking me in the eye.

We stay like that for a long time until she knows that I know she knows and that I know she loves me anyway.

Melissa and Debbie surprise me at the front door holding a bottle of Champagne and a camera. They've come to rescue me so that for a few hours I can feel like my old self, a teenager hanging out with my girlfriends on New

Year's Eve, with silly poses and smiles for the camera. We go up to my room and Debbie brings me up to date. Eileen's latest boyfriend is really cute and lives in Mamaroneck. Susan is back with her old boyfriend, who none of us like and wish she would have left him behind. Debbie is still working at her uncle's bar and restaurant, doing the books. She is really good at it. I envy how she knows exactly what to do, as though she's been doing it forever.

"School is okay, nothing new, Oh, except for the priest who now teaches religion. I think you'd really like him," Melissa says. "And I'm pretty sure that I'm going to the University of Bridgeport," she adds.

Melissa's parents told her to be a nurse and her father liked this university, so she's set. I wish my life was mapped out like that. I'm relieved when Debbie tells us she is going to work in the restaurant full time after graduation. She won't be leaving White Plains.

"With all that's been going on, I haven't been able to think about college or working or much of anything," I say.

"How are you doing with all of this? I mean, is adoption definite?" Melissa asks.

"I think so, it's so hard," I reply.

"Mr. Caven was here a few weeks ago and he's handling it; handling the adoption. I really don't have any choice. My parents aren't going to help me, and Scott doesn't seem to care about me anymore."

"Yeah, I heard he was back in White Plains and staying with friends, I'm not sure if he's in school or working," Melissa says.

"Colleen said she saw him with Joyce a few weeks ago," Debbie says, then wishes she hadn't.

"I'm not surprised," I say, my voice cracking.

"Can I touch your stomach?" Melissa asks.

"Yeah, the baby is kicking a lot lately," I tell them as they put their hands on my belly and the baby moves right on cue. We all giggle nervously.

"How does that feel, what's it like?" Debbie asks.

"It's amazing," I say. "Kind of like a butterfly fluttering, I can't describe it any other way."

"Hey let's go open the Champagne," I say after the baby settles down.

I take out the new crystal glasses my mother bought before Christmas and Melissa fills them. We clink our glasses.

"Thanks for coming tonight," I say.

This may be my best New Year's Eve. I thought I would be sad. I thought I'd go to bed early, so I wouldn't have to think about being alone. But I'm not alone, I have my friends. They'll never stop caring about me. They will always help me when I need them. I will never have to say goodbye to them.

———————

Next to Christmas, Super Bowl Sunday is the biggest holiday in our house. It's a combination of friends, football, food and alcohol, lots of alcohol. I've come to dread Super Bowl Sunday's arrival each year. I have been forced to serve, clear, wash, bring, fetch, stir and check on my father, who is usually passed out in some corner chair by half time. This is the first year I'm off the hook, and the first time in several months that I don't mind staying out of view. I'm a week past my due date, and I try not to think about what lies ahead. I turn on an old movie and prop my puffy body up. I doze off from time to time, occasionally awakened by the cheers and screams from the fans in our living room. Through my slumber I notice a dull pain. It comes and goes, and I'm pretty sure this is the beginning of labor. I don't want my baby to come now. Not on Super Bowl Sunday.

I use the bathroom in the middle of the night and see light spots of blood. I get back into bed not wanting to wake anyone. I fall in and out of sleep for a while until my father comes in and turns my light on. This is my signal to get up and drive him to the train station.

As he turns toward the door, I say, "I think I'm in labor."

"Does that mean you can't drive me?" he asks.

"I don't think I can," I reply.

The pain is getting longer and stronger, not as dull as it was through the night. I think these must be contractions that I'm riding. I go back into the bathroom and notice fluid trickling down my leg. On my way back, I stop in my mother's room, where she is still in bed.

"I think my water broke," I say.

"Okay, I'm getting up now," she says.

I know this will not be a dash to the hospital though. She is not a morning person and it doesn't help to try and hurry her along, so I get back into bed and wait. As the morning goes on, I begin moaning with the contractions. I get dressed as I hear my mother make her way downstairs.

"I'll call the doctor's office and see what they say," she says as she makes me tea. "Do you want something with the tea, maybe some graham crackers?"

"I don't think I'm allowed to have anything to eat," I say, "but I'm really hungry."

"Oh, this is very light," my mother says. "It should be fine."

I try to distract myself from the pain, by watching "Bewitched" while sipping the tea. I can't follow the plot, the pain is intensifying.

"Julie, how far apart are the contractions?" my mother asks.

"I haven't timed them, but they are coming up pretty quickly," I answer.

My mother, on the phone now, relays the information to the nurse and soon we are in the car, driving toward the office on this humid, rainy, dank, January morning. No blanket of freshly fallen snow, just melting piles, blackened by car exhaust; nothing beautiful about them.

We walk into the lobby and my mother sits on one of the benches.

"I'll wait for you down here," she tells me.

I take the elevator to the second floor then sit in the waiting room with all the other pregnant women who are going to keep their babies. I try not to show the pain. I don't want anyone to see me in labor; they may want to talk to me, maybe ask me questions. I quietly wait and try not to think about what will happen once my baby is born. I try not to imagine how my baby will be taken from me. I want to be pregnant forever.

I'm called into the examining room, where a doctor examines me. He is rough, and I remember he is the same doctor who first examined me at the free clinic. He's the same doctor who told me seventeen was too young to be pregnant, and once again I feel embarrassed and ashamed. He tells the nurse that I'm not dilated enough. He doesn't talk to me. When he leaves, the nurse tells me to go to the emergency room at the hospital. The doctor is ordering x-rays. I make my way down to the lobby, and my mother and I walk around the corner to the hospital. I'm put in a wheelchair and quickly taken to the x-ray room at the end of a long corridor. There is a small group of men standing outside one of the rooms, and I spot Scott's father. As I'm wheeled closer he sees me, but we don't say a word. I listen to their conversation and surmise that one of the construction workers was injured, and in the midst of all of this, I manage to recognize the irony. My thoughts are interrupted by another contraction. I'm helped onto the x-ray table. Bill Cosby will be my Lamaze coach. I decided that a couple of months ago when I saw him on a talk show. I can't remember what talk show, but he said Lamaze and I knew I should pay attention. I don't know exactly how Lamaze works, but he described labor like going up the mountain and then back down. I haven't climbed a mountain before, so I think of it more like riding the Dragon Coaster at Playland and all the while Bill Cosby is sitting next to me. I don't want to scream in pain, so I close my eyes and grip his hand, as the x-ray technician tells me to hold my breath and not to move.

I haven't seen my mother since I was taken to the x-ray room. I've asked the nurses if they can get her, but she isn't here yet. The contractions are getting stronger and I'm so tired. Too tired to cry. I want my mother and I want the doctor, but it's taking so long. Finally the doctor walks through the door with the news that the baby is in distress.

"We'll have to perform a c-section," he tells me.

"Oh, okay," I say through a contraction.

I don't know what distress means, but it sounds serious. And within moments there is a flurry of activity as I'm prepped for surgery and on my way to the operating room.

The fluorescent lights are blinding, the room cold. I didn't think I'd have a c-section. I don't understand why. Why is this happening? The anesthesiologist with his instruments neatly lined up, waits for me.

"Lean forward," his words feel harsh as he positions me.

Pressing me down, further, further. I can see the needle in my mind's eye, sharp, dangerous, searching for the spot to numb me. Nothing will numb my fear. No one to hold my hand. No one to say it will be okay, everything will be okay. Please, I need someone. There is nothing familiar here. The voices are muffled and distant. Doctors and nurses rushing by, hands bloody, and I know that soon I will meet my baby, the first step in saying goodbye.

CHAPTER SEVEN

THE MORNING AFTER MY baby girl is born, the sun is drenching the private room I'm in at the end of the hallway. It's away from the sound of newborn babies, boisterous friends and relatives who come to congratulate the proud new parents. My grief won't be noticed in my private room.

Three student nurses come in wheeling a bassinet. I'm going to finally hold my baby. One of the students in a loud whisper says, "she's not keeping her." My heart is breaking, I can't think about that now, we don't have much time together, my baby and me. I shuffle to the chair and when I'm finally settled, they hand me my daughter. I study her face for a long time. I tell the nurses that she looks like her father. She does. She has his eyes and dimpled chin. I can see him the way he was when I first saw him. I miss him. I wish he could see her too. I wish he would tell me everything is fine, let's take her home. I love you both. I'm not ready when a student nurse lifts the baby from me, so she's gone.

Each afternoon my mother visits and sits by my bedside knitting Christmas stockings. It's January, but this is my mother. She starts hiding gifts the year before and writes names and what's inside in shorthand on the back of the boxes. She has been doing this for as long as I can remember; always predictable. My mother writes lists and lists and more lists. She plans, prepares, and organizes. And yet here she sits knitting next to me; me a display of unpredictability. I was supposed to be a nice girl, who would graduate from her Catholic high school. I should have been visiting colleges, but instead I was a pregnant teenager. Now I am just a teenager with a future that has no face. So my mother has to knit and count and prepare for Christmas, smiling and cheerful, cheering me up, giving me moments of distraction. We can't talk about what is coming at the end of the week. We can't think about what is coming.

When my mother leaves I'm left to my own thoughts and fears. I can feel my breasts leaking. My milk is coming in, so I tell the nurse.

"Do you think I could breast feed the baby?" I ask.

"Oh no, she is already taking a bottle and, well, you won't be the one taking care of her, right?"

"Right," I answer.

So I use the tissues next to my bed to soak up my milk and to wipe my tears.

———————

Late in the afternoon, Debbie and Melissa come to visit me. I'm so happy to see them. They are my line to who I might still become.

"We just saw her, she's so beautiful Julie," Melissa says as Debbie smiles.

"She is, isn't she?" I say proudly.

"How do you feel?" Debbie asks, looking at the intravenous contraption.

"Oh I've felt better, but I'm getting there," I reassure her.

Then there is an awkward silence, followed by forced conversation that magnifies all the ways we are different now. I am consumed by thoughts of my baby and they can't even imagine it. I know that we will never be who we were together. It's clear that I'm not one of them anymore. It's clear to us all.

That evening, hooked up to the I.V., I manage to slide two chairs near mine as I wait for my parents' visit. Earlier I asked one of the nurses to bring the baby in when they get here. I'm not ready to let go. I'm not sure I can say goodbye. Maybe they will feel the same way. Maybe I can change their minds.

"Hey sweetie, how are you doing?" my father asks, giving me a kiss.

"I'm feeling much better than I did," I answer.

This is the first time I've seen him since the morning I couldn't drive him to the station. I never did find out how he got there. He is dressed in an Irish cable knit sweater and corduroy pants, looking very handsome as usual.

"You have your own room," he notices.

My mother sits across from me, takes out her knitting as my father positions his chair toward the television. Before I have a chance to tell them, the nurse rolls in the bassinet and parks it closest to my mother. Without a moment's hesitation, my mother picks up the baby and holds her with a knowing ease. Earlier in the day I tried to hold her but she fussed and fussed and cried and cried the entire time. Now I'm watching my daughter look up at my mother, soothed by her touch and her voice, eyes wide open and engaged. My heart is so full. My reality slips away as she is welcomed and admired and adored just like all the other babies. And for a short time, I'm a proud mommy just like all the other proud mommies.

"I don't think this is a good idea," my father warns, shifting in his chair. "We may get too attached."

"How could you think I wouldn't already be attached?" I ask.

Ignoring my question, he looks up at the television.

"I was attached long before she was born," I add.

But I don't want to waste a single moment with my precious baby, so I turn my attention to my mother's coos and kisses.

"I think she has the best of both of you, she's just beautiful," my mother decides. "And she is such an alert baby, so happy."

My father, noticeably uncomfortable, agrees that she is beautiful when my mother presses him.

"Would you like to hold her?" she offers.

Shaking his head he declines. My mother gently puts her in my arms. This time she doesn't fuss. Gingerly unwrapping her from her blanket, my mother helps hold her as I check her little hands and arms and her wiggly legs. I check her umbilical cord and hope that she'll have a nice belly button. I'm amazed at how perfect she is as I hold her tiny feet. We wrap her back up like a present, and I caress her dark hair ever so lightly.

"Dad, don't you want to hold her for just a minute?" I ask.

"No, no that's okay," he says.

It's clear to us all that my mother has already fallen in love and my father wants to avoid that trap. I hand the baby back to my mother so she can soak her up. When the nurse returns to take her to the nursery, I feel my mother's grief and my father's relief, and I wonder how I can possibly live without her.

The next afternoon, I'm feeling lonely when my mother comes in to show me the outfit she has bought for the baby to go home in. She is going to be a grandmother for only a brief time, so she is fitting in what she can. She went to B. Altman's and after narrowing down a few outfits, she decided on a pale pink and white embroidered layette. This is how she wants to send her out into the world. This is how she wants her new family to meet her. As long as I can remember, my mother has told me about the gaudy outfit she first saw me in. But she is quick to add, whoever put me in this thought I looked beautiful. She couldn't wait to get me into something soft and understated. I know this is my mother's way of telling me she loves me, and I know that this is her way of telling the baby how much she loves her.

It's Friday morning and I know it's just a matter of hours, maybe an hour, maybe minutes until my baby leaves the hospital. I saw her last night. I kissed her and said goodbye so quietly so neither one of us would hear it.

The phone rings and I hear my mother's voice on the other end.

"I've been crying in the shower. I thought I could come and help you when the lawyer comes, but I can't. I'm sorry."

"It's okay, I understand," I say.

When I hang up there is a man in a dark overcoat and hat stepping into my room. He is holding something, the papers. He tells me he is Mr. Caven's partner. I don't really see his face, just his hand that slides the bed tray up to me. The other hand is holding a pen. He says something to me, but I can't understand him. I tell him I can't do this. I'm sorry, but I just can't do this. Tears flowing, I see my father at the door.

"Dad, I can't do this, please," I beg.

My father is crying too, he can't come in the room; he is stuck in the doorway.

"Just sign here," says the man.

"I don't want this, please," I beg again.

"It'll be okay," my father says choking back his sorrow. "You have to."

I put the pen on the line and drag it across. I don't think I signed my name. I can't breathe, when I hear the nurse bringing in my baby. They have to match our bracelets. It's a procedure. But it's too cruel. I can't see her again.

"Don't bring her to me," I scream. "Please don't do this. Dad please don't let them do this."

I rip the bracelet off my arm and fling it toward the door. When I threw the bracelet it landed without a sound, but the silence would echo through the years.

PART II

Engagements, Weddings, Clomid, Lauren
and Sean

CHAPTER EIGHT

ON THE FLIGHT HOME FROM PARIS, I hesitate to drink the wine. I am positive I'm pregnant. I'm not. I'm certain it will happen next month. It doesn't. It just is going to take a while. I probably should go to a doctor. I do. He gives me Clomid. I know this is going to work. It doesn't. There's always Pergonal. I've heard they use the hormones from Catholic nuns to make Pergonal. No doubt it will work. Every morning I'm jabbed with a needle. My hormones are doing back flips. My breasts are sore, my stomach bloated and I hate my husband. It will be worth it. My HCG levels are not humanly possible. I'll have five babies. I don't. I'll try a specialist at Yale. They can get anyone pregnant. Not me. I try not to hope each month, but I do. The bright red drops swirl to the drain, and now I am really angry with God. "Are you telling me to adopt!?" I demand, then dry off and call Catholic Family Services to sign up for the mandatory adoption workshop.

I almost married once before. I was twenty-one, almost twenty-two. I really just wanted to get off the ride. The ride that would help me forget about my baby. It had been four years, and I still couldn't forget. They told me I would. That my life would be good. But I'd been on the ride of promiscuity, running from my pain, my memories ever since. Marriage would be my way to my parents' idea of success and salvation for my sins. I settled on a really smart lawyer who was into civil liberties, exposing the evils of society, legalizing marijuana and loving me. He was counsel for a state senator, so he split his time between Albany and Manhattan.

We spent our time in Brooklyn reading Mother Jones and Brecht, having sex and moving my car due to alternate side of the street parking regulations. He thought it would be a good idea to get married. So we did all the engaged things. Told our parents, picked a date. Chose a diamond that was to be set in platinum. He had lunch with my father in the city. Everyone was happy. Especially my grandmother. She would finally have a Democrat in the family. Someone who cared about politics. Someone who actually hated Reagan as much as she did. Someone who would agree how ridiculous it was for Nancy to change the perfectly good fine china at the White House. My grandmother kept all her birthday greetings from Tip O'Neill and was overwhelmed with pride when she heard my fiancé on CBS radio discussing the struggles of senior citizens. I let my mother choose the invitations, flowers, food. She found the wedding much more important than I did. I picked my bridesmaids. I chose a wedding gown, the first one I tried on. Ivory with a train. I didn't recognize the person in the three-sided mirror, but everyone thought I looked beautiful, so I put money down. It was to be a big church wedding. The reception in my parents' yard under a tent. His mother had asked about colors and my mother was making more lists than usual. Then on a sunny, end of the summer late morning, just a couple of weeks before the wedding, I pulled up to my parents' house with my friend, Matthew. I adored Matthew and would have preferred to spend the rest of my life with him if he wasn't gay and didn't plan to explore the world. He just had finished scolding me for not taking better care of the pearls that my parents had given me for my birthday that he found in the glove compartment.

"Julie, they're excavating!" Matthew shouted as we neared the back yard. "You've got to do something. Now!"

Matthew didn't like my fiancé and thought I probably didn't either.

So the next morning, I waited in front of the White Plains train station. My fiancé would be coming on the 11:05. We had planned a day of hiking, but I thought the best thing to do was to go to the meadow. It would be quiet there. Probably empty. I'd explain how I just wasn't ready, that we shouldn't see each other again, I'm so sorry, of course it was all my fault. He'd find someone better than me.

Later I watched as he climbed the stairs to get the 12:32 back to Grand Central. I spent another year on the ride until I married Peter. He was a good man; handsome, witty. I loved him and Matthew knew I did. That day I wore the pearls, the ivory gown and dyed to match pumps. And eventually my grandmother got over her Democrat.

Now I could have a baby. Now that I was married. This is the order of things. This is how it should work, according to God, according to my mother and father. It didn't matter that Peter wasn't much of a kid person. He'd go for one. He may, if I played it right, go for two. And I'm sure I didn't deserve more than that.

——— ——— ———

There are tables of ten. Five couples at each. We introduce ourselves and say how long we've been married. I think we are the youngest people in the group. I'm not thirty yet. Peter's just thirty-one. We have been married for six years. One couple has been married for more than seventeen years. I can't imagine it. Trying to have a baby for seventeen years. I'm sure that I will get pregnant any day now. This is a just in case. After infertility I'm left with a lingering fear of disappointment. I try to live without expectations. It's easier than being hopeful and then crushed. I'm approaching the adoption process with caution. During our mandatory adoption meeting, we are given the facts of the road that lies ahead. There are two speakers. One is a woman who has adopted a baby through this program. The other, a birth mother. This is the first time I have heard anyone describe the experience of giving up a baby. That was the language when she gave birth. She is about my mother's age. She shares her story by rote. She had no choice. She knows it was the best thing for everyone, is comfortable with her decision. Of course she wonders how her son is. She has a good life. I think everyone buys it. I don't buy it entirely. I can see that she has convinced herself. She can't live any other way. I feel sad for her. Here are two women. One is joyous, the other is not. The story becomes mechanical, methodical, but the pain is still there, always there.

Our phone call comes one year later.

"Julie, I just received a call from a social worker who is working with a young woman. She has read your profile and has decided that she wants you and Peter to be her baby's parents," Carolyn, our social worker, says.

Last summer on the way to Cape Cod, I wrote a profile. It is part of the adoption process. I included how fantastic we are, how interesting we are, that we have a loving family, wonderful friends, good jobs, education. The things I thought might matter.

"She loves the idea that Peter likes restoring old boats and cars," she continues.

"She does? Is that why she chose us? Are you sure she wants us? I mean is it definite?" I ask.

"Well of course she could change her mind, but I don't think that's going to happen," Carolyn assures me. "She is due next month, so you will have some time to get things ready," she adds.

"Her social worker would like to meet you and Peter. This birth mother is not comfortable with meeting directly with you," she continues.

"I can't believe this is happening. Thank you so much. When can we meet her social worker?" I say, anxious to get off and begin the phone brigade.

Everyone is thrilled. I'm thrilled. I can't be too thrilled. No baby showers. Please no baby showers. What if it doesn't happen? I'm afraid to decorate the room, except in my mind. I've been decorating and redecorating the nursery in my mind for years. Not yet. Not just yet.

It's the second Sunday in September. The baby was supposed to be born at the beginning of August. That's what the birth mother thought, that's what the social workers told us. Then the date was pushed further and further away. It is now past Labor Day and I'm sure that there is no baby. It was all a mistake. I'll have to get used to the idea. Be fulfilled in other ways. Maybe I'm just not supposed to be a mom. I spend the day flipping from acceptance to despair. And then the phone call comes.

A girl, eight and a half pounds. She has golden brown hair and pink skin. She's perfect.

Lauren Elizabeth. She's wonderful, barely cries, sucks down four ounces in no time, burps on command and sleeps through the night. During naptime I lie on the love seat with her on my chest. I stroke her back as she falls asleep. I rarely put her down. The autumn days are warm and sunny. I love showing her off, but I'm careful not to tell too many people she is adopted. I've had a good deal of stupid comments. The comments that sting. "She doesn't look adopted." "Did you meet the real mother?" "How could someone give away their baby?" "Now that you've adopted, you'll get pregnant." I suppose I could accept them as just curious or ignorant, but I'm very protective of my daughter, and I'm sensitive to anything that may hurt her. I understand how it must have been for my mother, the painful comments. I'm not sure much has changed since then.

It's been six weeks since Lauren was born. Carolyn calls to say that Lauren's birth mother has signed the papers to finalize the adoption. I am ashamed that I had a secret escape plan, conjured up during my sleepless nights when fear of her changing her mind would creep in.

"She asked if she could have a picture," Carolyn says.

Later that day, I pose Lauren in her cutest outfit propped up by a wall of stuffed animals, somehow trying to convey how much she is loved and cherished, knowing it isn't enough. I write a short letter thanking her for allowing us to be Lauren's parents. Thanking her seems so trivial, but I'm fumbling for the words that will fit. I tell her how bittersweet it is for me. I am feeling joy while I know she is feeling grief. I try to find some reason for the dichotomy. There is none. I hope the pictures will give her some happiness, some comfort and eventually a sense of peace. I want her to know I will always remember and love her.

CHAPTER NINE

I GRAB THE PHONE AFTER the fourth ring just before the answering machines picks up. It's Carolyn. She asks how Lauren is. I tell her that she is the most spectacular twenty month old God ever put on earth. Carolyn eases into her next topic about a baby boy who was born earlier that week. His birth mother is Asian and she and the birth father would like a family to adopt their baby who has some Asian background. Of course she thought of Peter with his Indonesian heritage. They also would like their baby to have a sibling. They would like to meet us first. There is another couple in the running, but I'm picking out names and redecorating Lauren's bedroom so it's perfect for a boy and a girl by the time I hang up.

Peter doesn't know that he has a son when he walks through the door. I tell him. He walks away from me and I follow him from room to room, telling him about our baby boy. He would have been fine without children. He is happy with one, completely in love with Lauren. Two? He can't wrap his head around it. I'm furious that it is taking him longer than thirty seconds to be excited by the idea of having a newborn in the house by next week. Of course that is if his birth parents choose us after our meeting.

———————

Today is one of those summer days that's neither warm nor cool, only heavy and humid, misting drops, suppressing my quick wit and confidence. I'm questioning my perfect mother outfit, as I peel the plaid skirt from my thighs. This is an audition for the role of a lifetime, and my thoughts are stifled by the weight of the air, as my perm gets tighter and tighter. We've been primed, rehearsed and I really want this part.

"You don't have to use your names, but it's up to you," Carolyn prepares us.

"Julie you can tell them that you are adopted and it would be a good idea to talk briefly about your Asian background, Peter. But don't go into too much detail, keep it simple," then adds, "I wouldn't mention anything about your giving up a baby for adoption, Julie."

The trip to the conference room is silent. Images swirl around me. All the perfect parents I've imagined. My baby's adoptive mother, who I've pictured roundish with dark brown hair, a warm smile and gentle touch holding my baby, her husband beaming with pride. A sudden image of my own young parents. The parents I know loved me and desperately wanted to keep me. And now there are two young parents waiting at the end of the hallway. But this isn't a fantasy, not in my head or dreams or desires. I understand that this is about being chosen and choosing and letting go and giving up and the pain returns. I wonder what we can say to them. How could it be enough? How can I be enough?

We take our seats in the cramped, fluorescent-lit office. I'm struck by this young woman's elegance and poise. She is wearing an angelic glow and all eyes rest on her. Not the overweight, water retaining young mother I expected, rather, petite and beautiful. Leigh gracefully introduces us to her boyfriend, Michael, as the social workers sit on the sidelines, to run interference or coach us along if necessary.

Michael has a huge personality that draws us in and relaxes us immediately. "Congratulations on your baby. I'm sure he must be adorable," spills from my mouth. Of course he is the most beautiful baby they've ever seen. *I know how hard this is. I can't believe how strong and brave you are. I've been through this too.* They have a list of questions for us. How long have we been married? Will we be married forever?

Our daughter at home, does she want a brother? Careers, dreams, hobbies, family, I hope we've answered them well.

Leigh, searching my face asks, "adoption, how will you tell..."

Interrupting I say, "I can answer any question your baby boy has, I'm adopted, I understand."

This makes them happy. I want to make them happy. I think they have already chosen us. I can see it in their faces. I want to stay here so the pain won't begin for her, won't be real. But it's time to leave.

Some "nice to have met yous" are exchanged, and then Leigh and I hug tightly.

"Love him," she whispers.

"I already do," I whisper back.

A few days later we walk into the Archdiocese building, up the long set of stairs and follow the high-pitched cries to find our baby boy in Carolyn's arms.

"Is that Sean's mommy?" Carolyn yells. I think he is the tiniest baby I have ever seen. He is almost too small to hold. I only see legs wiggling. I can't really see his face. It is twisted by his cries. Is he hungry? I take him and try a bottle. He isn't taking very much. I rock him and slowly he quiets. Lauren holds Peter's hand and announces that he is HER daddy. We have been a family of four for less than five minutes, and I can already feel the pull of my undivided attention.

Sean and I have been crying for several weeks. Peter's job has taken him away for much of the time, and I've broken every rule I vowed before having children, when I knew everything. The perfect bassinet that I put next to me lasted only a few days with both babies. Lauren grew out of it within a week and Sean is too wiggly. I have to free him from the top right corner every ten minutes. I'm afraid to bring him into bed with me for fear I may squish him, or he may squirm off the edge. He is now in his crib and Lauren is in my bed. I don't know yet that she will never want to leave. She was practically potty trained when we brought Sean home. Now she not only wants to wear a diaper, she wants a newborn diaper. It will only fit around her leg. It's okay. It makes her happy. Her juice bottle is filled at all times. This also makes her happy. I never think about my children being adopted. I'm just in the middle of motherhood and all of its rewards.

I haven't felt sleep deprivation before. Not really. Sean can only drink one ounce of formula at a time, spends the next hour sleeping, and then wakes screaming. And so it goes. During his feedings we slowly go back and forth in the rocking chair. He looks up with his brown eyes and I sing "Hush Little Baby." We have conversations about time. What is time? Does time really matter? If I learn to meditate can I, in fact, eliminate sleep? He has soulful eyes and I'm sure he knows the answers to all of these questions. I burp him and put him down for another hour.

On a particularly tear-filled day, we take a drive to the CVS Pharmacy. I hold him up to the pharmacist as an offering and ask him to help us. Beg him to make him stop crying. He points us to the formula that costs more than our entire grocery bill. He mentions the same drops that the pediatrician had prescribed weeks before. No relief.

———

Peter's parents hadn't been supportive of adoption. They hadn't been supportive of our marriage either. There was an angry telegram from them that arrived just days before the wedding forbidding the marriage. His parents would not attend. In the years that followed I had written letters, sent cards, pictures. Thought all was forgiven, until a little man no more than five foot two inches tall came marching toward me at the Kennedy Airport arrival gate. We were the third leg of his journey from Indonesia. This was my first meeting with my father in law. He brushed past Peter and asked if I was Julie. I was certain he was going to tell me how wonderful it was to meet me. Before I could answer he ranted at how I ruined his wife's life. He couldn't describe how upset she was. Peter tried to prepare me for his father's eccentric, hysterical ways. Looking to Peter to be rescued, he shrugged and without saying a word told me *this is what I meant, this is why I haven't seen him in eight years.* It would be another few years until I met Peter's mother, an American from the south. She was kind, funny, and I could see the good traits of Peter in her. But adoption was something not to be spoken of. When she learned that I was adopted she didn't believe me. I quickly understood she did not have good feelings about adoption. Passing down bloodlines was important to both of Peter's parents.

Then Lauren and Sean were born. Peter's father called Lauren 'the little girl' and Sean 'the baby.' I wasn't sure but I thought I sensed a touch of warmth. But with his mother I could see the years of southern provincial thinking subside, reverse, disappear. She became their Grandma from far away, who lived on a mountain top in Indonesia, killed snakes with a broom, wrote endearing stories for them, had exotic birds, goats, a zillion cats and banana trees in her yard. Love prevailed. We became a family.

PART III

Sealed Records, Search Manual, Yonkers and Pat

CHAPTER TEN

THE AFTERNOON SUN SPILLS across the cocoon of blue plaid couches, hand painted ducks and wood signs that welcome friends. The coffee maker spits, and I pour a cup before it's ready. The brass-handled doors are open on the oak clawed foot chest, where the television has captivated my attention away from the photographs waiting to be organized into a quilted album. Another reunion show. Maybe it's the happy faces or tears of joy that draw me from the shelter of my closed mind, from the well-rehearsed lines I pull up on cue, the perfected performance. I don't want to know. I'm sure I don't want to know. I'm really fine not knowing. But before the show ends, I've dialed the number flashed across the screen, and hold for the next available operator, lullabied by Linda Ronstadt and Aaron Neville insisting that somewhere out there someone's thinking about me, credit card readied for my how to search manual.

It takes the UPS truck just two days to deliver the enormous three-ringed binder, "A Guide to Searching," complete with tips and pages and pages of forms. I need a partner in my detective work, so I call the one person I know won't talk me out of it, my friend, Melissa. The year we turned thirty, Melissa and I had dinner in Little Italy and toasted to the next decade. "Don't worry Julie, this year we'll find you a baby," she said lifting her glass. "And we'll find you a man," I added raising mine. I couldn't have known then we would also find my birth mother. Melissa is a fellow mystery reader; she and I have been on a P.D. James streak. I am confident she will approach this challenge with intrigue and vigilance. I have our time line, place of birth, the name of the adoption agency and age of my birth mother. I am certain this will not be impossible. I will not be deterred. The search begins.

The voice at the other end tells me that I have reached Westchester Adoption Agency.

"I'm not sure if you can help me. I, I," I begin interrupted by a flood of sobs.

"Take your time," the voice says.

"I was adopted, and I'm sorry I don't know why I'm crying," I manage.

"It's okay, take as long as you need."

"Information, I just would like to know something about my birth parents."

The Westchester Adoption Agency is now located in a storefront, nothing like the stately brick colonial where I met with the social worker nearly a generation of Wednesdays ago. I have Lauren by one hand as I push the stroller with the other down Mamaroneck Avenue, through the heavy doors and down the hallway to, Pamela, the social worker's office. She and I spoke briefly on the phone, but in that short time, I felt a connection.

"Mommy has a meeting, so I need you guys to play quietly," I say, taking Sean out of the stroller.

Lauren dumps the toys and crayons and books from the red bag that we never leave home without.

"Julie, I've pulled your file. Hmm let's see what we have," Pamela begins.

"Their names, just their first names," I suggest.

She can't.

"Initials, just initials. I'll guess and you can nod," I say.

She can't.

"I can spend time going through the file and send you a report with non-identifying information," she says, scanning the pages.

"It says that your birth mother made no further contact with the agency."

No further contact. I try to ignore the harshness of those words as Pamela hands me a form from a reunion registry somewhere in Nevada.

"They have had some luck with this, International Soundex, I'm sorry that I can't do more," she says.

I believe she is.

I want to include my parents in the search for my birth mother. I've been rehearsing the conversation in my mind for a week and find myself across from my mother at her kitchen island. I'm shielded by the mountain of newspapers, vitamin bottles, boxes of tissue and newly folded dish towels that have no other place to go. There is no denying that this monster of a kitchen island is too big for this room. My mother doesn't seem to notice. She designed this kitchen. She doesn't have the space she did in our old house. The house we rebuilt. The house where fire screamed through the halls and up the staircases, shattering its beauty, its charm, its history. Then my parents moved to Connecticut and this house began as a blank slate, but quickly became stained by drinking and fighting, and ugliness began to seep into its walls too.

"Mom," I say.

"Yes," she answers picking her head up from her paperwork.

"I've decided to contact the agency you adopted me from."

"Oh," she says with a look of shock.

"Only non-identifying information. You know, medical information. That sort of thing," I say, hoping to eliminate the sudden onset of anxiety that seems to be taking over her.

"Don't tell Dad, he'll be very hurt," she says, pretending to put her attention back on her paperwork.

"I won't," I say, understanding that this conversation is over.

The adoption process was veiled in secrecy when I was a baby. She knows that I have met my son's birth parents. This frightens her. How could I meet them and still be his mother. Our experiences are too different, too foreign.

Late in the week, I receive a call from Pamela, the social worker from the adoption agency.

"I have good news," she announces.

I know she's changed her mind and will tell me everything.

"I spoke with your foster mother," she continues.

"My foster mother?"

I hadn't thought about a foster mother.

"She has a picture of you at six weeks. She remembers you and wondered how you turned out."

"She does? I mean she has a picture of me? She remembers me?"

"You were with her for a month or so," she continues.

"What is her name?" I ask.

"Oh, I'm sorry, I can't give you her name," she answers.

Not long after our call, I receive the picture. Faded by the years, a tiny baby on a bed, a script of pencil on the back, Frances, 1958.

———

Records of an adoptee are altered everywhere. Adoptees in New York State are not permitted to see their original birth certificates, and, I recently learned, not their original baptismal certificate either. But the "Guide to Searching" manual suggests writing to the church anyway and maybe they will slip up with some names for me. Melissa and I put it on our list, along with the International Soundex form that Pamela gave me at our meeting, the huge database that hopes to match adoptees with their birth families. But now it's all beginning to seem like an outside chance.

The baptismal certificate does come, delighting Melissa and me. Our first victory of sorts. I was baptized at St. Augustine's Church in Ossining, NY. My original name isn't on the certificate, but the names of my original godparents are. They have Italian names, Carmella Grieco and Luciano Siri. Melissa is pretty sure they knew my birth mother. Just a feeling. I have the thought that I could be the daughter of a Mafia don, making me a Mafia princess waiting to be discovered. Maybe I was with my foster mother then. But she didn't have me for long. Everything goes into the anything is possible category. I wonder about my godparents. Do they still have a picture of me? Do they remember me? Melissa takes on the task of trying to locate them. I'm not sure why, but I don't think I'm ready to learn what they may know.

Sometime after the baptismal certificate and the baby picture of Frances, Pamela's report arrives. The information we covered in the office, my weight in grams, condition at birth. And news of another placement. Another family. I was originally placed with an Italian family in Ossining, but suddenly without explanation taken away from that home. She can't say why. So, I continue reading.

The caseworker described your mother as attractive, with a nice smile and dimples; your grandmother as a stern woman who accompanied your mother by taxi to the agency. Your grandmother didn't say too much but described your father as being pleasant of face with a strong shouldered walk. He played the drums, she loved to read, he had asthma, she loved to dance. She was Irish American, he was Italian American. His mother was born in Italy. He lived there for a time. She named you Donna.

CHAPTER ELEVEN

I'M READY TO HANG UP the phone and say no thank you, when the man says something about International Soundex database in Nevada. I almost forgot I had filled out this form, it seemed like a long shot. He asks me to verify my birth date and hospital where I was born. He has found her. My birth mother. Her name is Patricia. She is from Yonkers. Yonkers! She has three children. Oh, my God, she has three children! He gives me their names, and I write them down on the back of an envelope. He tells me I was born at 1:01 pm and I tell him that is wrong. I was born at 3:00 in the afternoon. He reminds me that this is the information that my birth mother has given so it is probably more accurate. He will call her today and tell her about me. I'm not so sure this is a very good idea. I'm okay with just this information. He tells me that she filled out her form several years ago. She wants me to know her. I tell him to call.

The next morning as I wait for the phone to ring, I pace around the house, room to room, busying myself with vacuuming, laundry, dusting. I clean when I'm terrified.

When it rings, I drop the mop and grab the phone from the wall.

There's a whisper of a voice on the other end, and suddenly I am strong.

"It's okay, I'm happy; I've had a really good life, really," I say.

"Do you have any children?" she asks.

Here it is. I know it's all so complicated, but I just want to get this out of the way.

"Two. We adopted our kids, and, well I have been through what you have. I, I had a baby and gave her up."

"I'm sorry," she manages.

Surely I have scared her off and ruined any chance of our being together. This may be all I get.

"Your father's name was Donald. He died. He was only twenty-two when he died," she says.

"Oh he was so young," I say, but I really only want to talk about her.

"Can I see you?" I ask, trying not to sound desperate.

"I think I should send you some pictures first and then we can meet after that," she offers.

Disappointed I agree that would be best, but I really think it's a terrible idea. I'd much rather drop everything and meet her today.

After a few endless days, I lock myself in the bathroom and open the large envelope with the return address of my birth mother. Oh my God, she's blonde! Blonde! We have the same eyes. Hers are blue. Mine are brown. They are the same eyes though. She is really beautiful. More beautiful than I could have imagined. There are throngs of relatives. Siblings. Grandparents. Cousins. There is a stepfather. I study their faces. Her brothers all seem to have the same forehead as me. Her father's chin is identical to mine, or mine is identical to his. I study each picture through tears. I'm crying because I was left out. I wasn't on the couch with Pat and her children, my siblings, as they smiled for the camera. I wonder what I would have worn to her parents' anniversary party. I missed opening presents on Christmas Day as her brothers looked on. I never had a chance to dance in the living room as Pat cheered. I am overcome with grief. I never expected this. I'm not looking for a new family. I love my family. I just wanted to know why I look like I do. That is all it is, no more than that. Why does this hurt so much? How can I love her so much?

We decide to meet on Pat's birthday. It's been fifteen days since the phone call from the International Soundex man. Now I am sure I am having a panic attack, hands sweaty, breathing shallow. Or maybe I'm having a heart attack. I can't tell. I didn't picture it this way. Meeting Pat, the mother who gave birth to me. City streets, malls, beaches, airports, I looked in all those places, studied the faces, but she will be in my living room, here, today, and I will never have to wonder again. I see the white Cadillac slowing in front of the door. Within moments, without words I'm in her arms. She doesn't let go. I don't want her to ever let go.

Our husbands don't quite know what to do with us, forcing us to make introductions, small talk, weather talk, job talk, kid talk. She is even prettier in person, wearing jeans, a light blue button down blouse and a camel blazer. I wish her a Happy Birthday and give her the photo album I've been working on. A glimpse of my life, since she last saw me. Moments in time. My first Christmas with my dog, Penny. Standing in the snow with my fur-trimmed coat, flanked by one brother on each side, wearing my beanie that goes with my bright blue school uniform. First Communion, Confirmation, my favorite Easter outfit, graduation, wedding day. I think it's not enough. It doesn't say what I mean, what I intended. I'm new at this. Clumsy.

"Mommy, Mommy," my little ones yell running toward me, arms outstretched. Pat is enchanted. My sister follows and gives a quick report on the fun they had at the park. She, too, doesn't know what to do with us and leaves just moments later. Tearing into the gifts their new friend Pat has given them, the children bring us together. Give us a place to look, a place to hide, a place to slow the swirling that is raging inside us both. She smiles when the last candle is blown out, and I hope I will see her again.

———

Our second meeting is at a restaurant in Mt. Kisco, a town halfway between Yonkers and Connecticut. I find a spot a few stores down. Pat is waiting for me on the sidewalk in front of the restaurant, and from this distance I can see that we are built the same, stand the same, hold our hands the same. She's nervous. I'm in love. We are seated at a small table next to a tray of dishes, so I demand another table. It seems to me that Pat doesn't notice this detail. But all I notice now are details, her big smile, laugh, dimples, eyebrows. I don't know what we are. I feel different when I'm with my girlfriends. I know them better. It's easier with them. It's easier with my mom. I'm not my best self right now. I can't stop asking questions, questions and more questions. "When did you get your first period? Do you gain weight in your butt first? Do you love chocolate? What books have you loved the most? When did you go blonde?"

I ask Pat to tell me the story about how she and my birth father met. She indulges me. I'm not sure if everything is accurate, but I press her for details and she provides them. She tells me about the afternoon she and her friends walked past his house.

"What were you wearing?" I ask.

"Jeans and loafers," she answers.

He was really handsome and began to flirt with her. I like to think that it was love at first sight. They spent the summer together at Tibbets Park in Yonkers. She remembers that he was an impressive diver and everyone loved to watch him. When I was a child, I would picture my birth mother in a 1950's white and black dress, strapless with a crinoline slip while my birth father, in a white dinner jacket and black bow tie, drove them in a shiny red convertible to a dance. There, they danced and danced and all eyes were on them. I'll have to get used to the true version of summer love at the pool.

"I'm okay with just a picture of my birth father," I say.

She has assured me that with her Yonkers' connections, husband the detective, son the city worker, a picture shouldn't be a problem to find.

"If they can't find a picture, did he look like Sal Mineo?" I ask. "I've always suspected that he looked like Sal Mineo."

"I think he did. Yes," she agrees, making the comparison in her mind.

"I thought so," I say with confidence.

I'm happy to picture Sal Mineo with a strong-shouldered walk.

"I brought some pictures of my family," I say, tugging the envelope from my bag. I'm excited to show Pat a family picture that was taken recently, my parents, brothers, spouses, grandchildren. This will prove to her how happy my life is, my childhood was. This will prove it to us both. But we don't look at them. She can't.

"I love your mother, though. I just can't look at her. I don't have to meet her to know that I love her," she explains.

Next time I'll be more careful.

———

For my thirty-fifth birthday, Pat and her husband, Tom, want to take Peter and me somewhere special, a steakhouse in Brooklyn. I don't eat steak, but I hear the excitement in her voice and tell her we'd love to. We meet at their apartment in Yonkers. It's up high on the banks of the Hudson River. If you stand on the balcony and look to the left you can see the George Washington Bridge. I'm fascinated by apartment buildings. All those lives lived under one roof. My grandparents lived in an apartment. I loved riding the elevator and throwing their trash away in the incinerator right across the hall. My brothers, sister and I would fight over whose turn it was to pull down the shoot. Pat's apartment feels spacious. I'm taken aback by the cowboy theme in the living room though. Must be her husband's idea. Pat wants me to sit down and open some gifts before we go to the restaurant. Tucked inside a flowered hatbox, a runner of antique lace is wrapped around a delicate hand painted pitcher.

"Your great - great grandmother brought them from Ireland," she tells me.

And inside the pitcher, a letter dated August 4, 1900 to my great - great grandmother from her nephew apologizing for not being able to see her while he was in New York. He is staying at the Vanderbilt on Lexington Avenue. I am reading a piece of my history. Words from my ancestors. Next I open the small wrapped box and carefully take out the Claddagh gold cross. It's a replacement for the one that Pat put on me when she brought me to the adoption agency. I never knew about that, until now. The swirling continues. Who was I, who will I become?

On the way to the restaurant, I ask Pat to show me Dana House. I had learned Pat spent the last few months of her pregnancy at Dana House, a home for unwed mothers. I'm happy they don't say that anymore. Unwed mothers. We drive through the Upper East Side of Manhattan and slow down on 72nd Street, while Pat tries to recognize the home that she and I shared for the first two weeks of my life. It is now owned by one of the city's elite residents. She remembers her daily walks through the Metropolitan Museum of Art. I love the Metropolitan. I have always felt a pull toward the halls and walls of that museum.

"That's it I think. The stone white building," she says.

We pull up as close as possible and double park. I want to get out of the car and walk up the stairway, hold the railings. Try to imagine. But Pat is stuck in time and can only look through the back seat window.

"Your birth father and his brother came to see us here. He held you and told me we would get married," she remembers.

"I didn't know," I say.

Her eyes fixed to the second floor window she continues, "he told me his mother would cook for me. Then he kissed us both goodbye."

He didn't marry her though, his mother didn't cook for her and so we drive away in silence.

There are several ways to get to Brooklyn. We have to go over the Williamsburg Bridge, but I think we passed it. Maybe Pat's husband, Tom, knows a different way. I don't think this is the way. We are in Chinatown. That's the Manhattan Bridge and I know we don't want the Brooklyn Bridge. Should I give directions? Nobody is asking me. So I just sit back and talk to Pat about her children. Her two daughters are in their early thirties and her son will be thirty soon. She has told them about me. Two out of three are intrigued by the idea of a surprise sister. One of her daughters would rather not meet me just yet. Pat doesn't think she will tell her parents or brothers about me. I can see the shame that is still attached to me, but I don't have to think about that now. I just want to think about us, Pat and me. My birth mother and me in the back of a Cadillac, looking for Brooklyn on my birthday.

Pat has invited us to meet her children. Well two out of three, Kim and Anthony. Neither are married, no children. Peter and I decided to bring the kids and tell them we are going to see our new friends, Pat and Tom. They are too young to understand. I don't understand. My mind is not wrapping around the idea that I am meeting my half-brother and half-sister today. I don't know if I'll feel a connection. I wonder what they'll think of me. They just learned about me a few weeks ago. My stomach has been flipping the entire ride down to Yonkers. I'm trying to appear happy, at ease, but I don't know if I can pull it off. We find a parking space right in front of the building. There is a meter, so we'll have to remember to feed it every few hours. We don't spend much time in cities so the kids are really excited about going to an apartment way up high in the sky. We decide before entering the elevator that Lauren will push the button to go up to the apartment and Sean can push the button to go down when we go home. I'm feeling that newly familiar wave of anxiety as we approach Pat's apartment. Standing at the door to welcome us is Pat with Anthony and Kim behind her.

"She looks so much more Guido then I thought she would," Kim blurts out.

I don't know how to respond to that so I don't say anything. Pat giggles nervously as Anthony smiles and puts his hand out to shake mine. I'm sure he feels as awkward as I do, so I quickly introduce the kids and hope they will serve as a much needed distraction. They do. These are definite kid people. Anthony and Kim show them the balcony and the Hudson River. They can see the pool where we are going to swim after lunch. There is a spread covering the dining room table, enough to feed everyone twice. The conversation is a get to know you chat. Where do you live, work, play, where did you go to school. I can see that we are studying each other as we talk, only half listening. Soon Kim is telling me about aunts and uncles and now my head is spinning. I'm relieved when the kids begin to beg for the pool. We all need a change of scene, and I need a task. Bathing suits, sun block, swimmies. The pool will provide us with some down time. Time to forget about why we are here. Soon Pat and I are in the pool with the kids, while the others are talking and laughing on the deck. And suddenly there is a collective ease among us. I'm not sure I feel like I've just met my brother and sister. But I know that I met these really good people in Yonkers who already love my kids.

My real life interrupts the new elation and romance I've found with my birth mother. The complication of this affair is more than I had bargained for. With my mother's words echoing, "don't tell your father." I plummet into the world of deceit. One more sin. The love isn't multiplying the way it does when you have more children, it's divisive and painful and selfish. I'm very cautious when I see my parents now. Careful not to blow my cover. I cringe when Lauren tells my mother about our visit to Pat and Tom's "compartment" building with the swimming pool and the elevator. And like any adulterer, I am quick with a lie. Our visits are lessened and quieter and stifled. I don't know if they detect this or if I see them differently. I want to tell them. I want them to all meet. I want them to say, "We all love you, and this is all going to work out." But this is not the case. I am obligated to this family. My family. I don't think I fit in Pat's family. Did I really find something or am I losing everything?

It's our first Christmas. I always take time and put thought into giving gifts. I want to tell the person I notice them, think about them. My first Christmas with Pat is exhausting. I know so much about her past, incidents of her life, but I don't really know her. This is obvious when I set out to find the perfect gift. The gift that says I've known you all along. This is what you've been waiting for. I scan store after store, bookstores, jewelry stores, department stores. Some are too personal, some not enough. Then there is her family. I really don't know them. They don't know me. Everything is new. We are trying to jump into a state of harmony. I try. They try. She says she loves the white sweater. I tell her I love mine. We settled on the same thing. Not quite right. It's a moment to be relived again and again. Not quite right.

On a misty Saturday in May, Pat gives Sean and me a tour of my roots. At two, Sean has a limited amount of words, so I know that the day's events will be kept quiet. Yonkers, this is where it all began. Yonkers has always been off the radar for me. I never imagined a birth mother in Yonkers. It is separated from the rest of Westchester County by those who live in the rest of Westchester County. I'm not proud of my snobbery on this point and know that few people will admit this. We first drive to the neighborhood where my birth father lived. Where they first saw each other. The house is gone. Most of the houses are gone. But I can see Pat walking down the steep hilled street, Donald, my birth father, leaning on the railing of his front porch. She is giggling with some friends when he catches her eye. He thinks she is the cutest girl he has ever seen and entices her to come back. No trees, old cars, cement piles where buildings once stood. And yet, I can feel their attraction, their innocence.

A few short blocks away, we pass the warehouse where Donald died. Melissa in her perfected detective work had located his obituary and death certificate. He died of carbon monoxide poisoning. It was considered an accident. Melissa and I have our doubts. He was working as a chauffeur at the time and Pat believes he was cold on that November evening when he climbed in the back seat and fell asleep.

Next we move down toward the river to find St. Mary's Street, the street Pat grew up on. Pat hated her house. It's older than any house I've ever seen, not the charming old kind, but the falling down, depressing kind. I catch Pat as she is visiting her painful memories. I leave her to her thoughts and wait in the car.

There is a lovely section in Yonkers that gets overlooked, and this is where Donald's mother now lives. We pull across the street from her freshly painted house with its manicured lawn. I would have liked to have known my Italian family. Maybe I will knock one day. Maybe I won't complicate things anymore. Am I getting in too far? I pull away slowly, taking in the strange familiarity of this block.

As we drive toward the parkway, Pat suggests we go to the cemetery where Donald is buried. I agree, but I really am not one to visit cemeteries. Maybe this is something she wants to do, needs to do. Her other children's father is buried just a few rows down from Donald. And there are Donald's brother and father next to him. All in the ground. I pretend to say a prayer, because I'm sure most people would say a prayer at their father's grave. Faster than is probably respectful, we are off to visit Tibbet's Park, where their love and I took shape.

It's been almost two years since our reunion and it's getting easier to spend time with my other family. We're seated at a table by the bay windows of a quaint, white clapboard restaurant not far from my house, as snow flurries swirl. The room is aglow by candlelit tables and a fire in the fireplace. Tom, my new stepfather, can talk more than my new sister, Kim. He's a detective. A Yonkers's detective; with a handle bar mustache and exaggerated New

York accent. I'm fascinated by his stories, but my new brother, Anthony, gives me a look that assures me this isn't the first time he's heard it. Kim excuses herself and steps outside for a cigarette. I guess she's heard it too.

"I was there when they brought the Son of Sam in."

The Son of Sam. He's talking about the Son of Sam, who terrified us all the summer of 1977. One night, sitting outside of the diner in my car with my friend, Patti, a sudden wave of fear took over us. We both had long dark hair, the long dark hair that would be a target for this Son of Sam. The terror pushed us down to the floor.

"Yeah the night he was arrested," he continues.

"And the Carr brothers, their dog who told him to kill those people, did you know them?" I ask.

"Oh yeah, probably heard the dog barking too," he says, taking a swig of beer.

My family doesn't have any stories like this. The only one that comes close is the one about my grandmother's brother who was shot as he hung on the running board of a car. Something to do with prohibition. That was in the 1920's. My grandmother would never discuss it.

Tom slides into another story of a case he was lead detective on. A murderer who fled to Columbia. Then I remember I've seen Tom before. He was interviewed on

America's Most Wanted. Only I didn't know he was my new stepfather then. I feel the shift now. These are new memories we are all making, together. I think I now know enough about how I got here. The conversation turns to my brother Anthony and his classmate, John Gotti, Jr. Really? He went to school with John Gotti, Jr.?

———————

Summer has finally arrived and Pat and I are playing golf later this week. I'm not surprised to see Pat's name on the caller ID. I know she is firming up the plans.

I quickly say, "Hi Pat."

There are sounds of grief on the other end.

"Julie, Kim died. They think she had an aneurysm."

I can't speak for a few moments, then I tell her I'm so sorry and I love her and I'm here if she needs me. She doesn't have any details on the arrangements yet.

The last time I saw Kim, was a hot humid night. We were sitting on my patio drinking cold beer. She was wearing a flowing white dress with her long wavy hair, she looked particularly beautiful. It was a night of talk of the Yankees, her new car and Naples.

Tom, my new stepfather, calls with the information for the wake and funeral. I thank him, but I already know I won't be going. Pat's mother, her daughter, the one who doesn't want to know me just yet, and her brothers, who don't know I exist will be there. There are sisters in-law, nieces, nephews, cousins, friends. I'd have to sneak in the back, be anonymous. So I send flowers and spend the hour of the funeral at a Grotto of the Virgin Mother. I light a candle, write Kim's name in the book of intentions and hope that she knew that she was important to me. I'm regretful that we didn't have a chance to become closer. I didn't see her new apartment. We didn't hang out in the city, and we missed our chance to eat our way down the Amalfi Coast.

PART IV

*School Plays, City Trips,
Breakdowns and Belia*

CHAPTER TWELVE

I'M ON THE COUNTDOWN to forty, and I've been noticing babies again. This could be my last chance. When I was going through infertility treatments, the doctors never found anything wrong. At the time I thought that was a bad thing. If there was something wrong they could fix it. Now it makes me hopeful. I decide to just check it out with another doctor. Can I possibly go through any of that again? What about Peter? He doesn't want to adopt again. I know that. He doesn't share my enthusiasm and look of want when I tell him about the beautiful baby girls in China who are being adopted by American families. Maybe he would be willing to try just one more time to get pregnant. I make an appointment without telling him. I feel drained having to fill out the paper work, explain to the doctor the tests I had undergone, the medication, unsuccessful treatments. I tell the doctor that we adopted two children. He tells me one of his children is adopted, and I know I'm in for the count your blessings speech. I'm right. He continues to tell me that if I haven't become pregnant spontaneously by now it will more than likely not happen. We'd have to do in-vitro. I get it now. This is my family. I let it go. I go home and tell Peter what I did that day. He gives me a consoling hug. I'm sure that he is relieved that my quest is over. But we would soon learn that our family would be changed once again.

CHAPTER THIRTEEN

MY PARENTS HELD ON TO the letter for several weeks. The mailbox stands at the end of the road. Half dirt, half paved. Now that he is retired, my father journeys down each afternoon to collect his mail and newspaper, never alone, dog or grandchild by his side. He doesn't recognize the return name. Belia Marie, somewhere in the Bronx. She thinks he is her biological granddaughter. She wants to know about me. She won't interfere. She just wants me to see the pictures and give her some medical history. He doesn't want to know this, doesn't want to be involved. He was sure this, this situation was long gone. Forever forgotten, never to be discussed. He's not sure he'll tell my mother, but of course he does. She will decide if I should know.

***

The pressure is enormous when an eight year old dances. It's nearly impossible to compete with the bobby pin, hairspray-toting mothers. The mothers with the costume changes, perfectly aligned on rolling wardrobes. I'm keenly aware of my mediocre costuming skills, as I struggle to sew sequins, so my bumblebee can buzz for tonight's performance. The sound of the doorbell snaps me out of my concentration, but I'm more than surprised, confused, to see my parents huddled on the front stoop. Did someone die? I think I should ask as we scurry into the kitchen. My mother begins to empty a plastic grocery bag filled with mismatched plastic containers, magazines that have very important articles, free Christmas cards that came from St. Jude's with her donation, all items she knows I must need. But my father in my kitchen on a Friday afternoon handing me an envelope?

"What's this?" I ask.

I scan the page and the pictures. A little girl with dark hair, receiving a certificate from a nun, maybe kindergarten graduation? A teenager with long flowing dark hair and an expression that looks like me. I think this is my daughter and she thinks she is my father's biological granddaughter and I've never heard her name before and she lives in the Bronx. And Scott, what about Scott?

I put the envelope down and pick up the costume.

164

"I'm surprised by your reaction," my mother says, "I thought you'd be more excited, more..."

"I, I can't think about this right now, I have to finish sewing on the sequins."

——— —— ——

Our first call was shortly after I wrote Belia back. Tucked away downstairs, I freeze as I hear her voice. I should have thought about what I would say to her. I can only ask if she is happy. She tells me that her parents are dancers. Her parents are dancers, but I want to know about her. She grew up in Queens and Long Island. I had always pictured her living in a big house in Northern Westchester. Probably Yorktown Heights, with a pool and swing set. She is describing crack houses, subways and dancers. I ask about her sister, Jennifer. That's not her name. But they told me it was Jennifer. She asks about her birth father, and we talk about the Rolling Stones, and I don't know what I'm saying.

Then I remember to ask, "how did you find me?"

"My uncle was with my parents the day they picked me up from the lawyer's office. There was a torn hospital bracelet sitting on the table. He picked it up, read your name, then put it in his pocket. He thought God had something to do with it."

The bracelet. My baby. The bracelet. Now I'll have to relive it, remember it all, but I don't know if I can.

———————

I'm three, almost four weeks into my new position of reunited birth mother. From this side, the relationship is rooted in memories. Places my mind couldn't tour. I'm treading on the present, daring to hope for a future. My words are careful, my actions more so. I look to Pat as a mentor. I'm ashamed at how I poked and prodded her for my benefit, my curiosity. Belia is no different, calling me several times a day, for more answers and new questions. I'm exhausted by it all, when she announces one morning that she and her boyfriend are driving up. She's ready to meet me. There's no time to get my hair blown out. No time to obsess over what to wear. And the kids? Babysitter? Pledge the furniture, vacuum, food? Not like my first reunion.

Two hours late. I've given up waiting inside and think she will get there sooner if I sit on the step near the driveway. It works, and I glide to her car as she drives up. She takes a moment to open the door. Our hug is too quick, a slight brush as she asks to use the bathroom. I only catch a glimpse.

My voice is muffled by the weight of the visit. The thoughts are fleeting, and I'm left without much to say. I recognize Scott in her face. She does the same thing with her mouth that he did, bites her lip on one side. I had forgotten about that. She has dark eyes and long dark hair like me. She bought her dress in the men's department at Macy's, and our pinky toes match.

———

"I found Scott. I left him a message and he called me back," Belia excitedly tells me.

The honeymoon is over. I have to share her. She is going to see him tonight. He lives in Manhattan, in Chelsea. I don't want to know this. I'm suddenly filled with jealousy.

"That's great," I manage, pushing my voice up.

I don't want her to find out I'm anything but loving, accepting, understanding.

"Have fun and we'll talk tomorrow."

He has the nicest city apartment she has ever seen. He's wonderful. He's single and has a fabulous life. They talked all night. He's going to take her to dinner. He is exceptionally good looking, looks ten years younger than he is. I've suddenly spiraled from cheery, to fake cheery, passing sadness, directly to hatred. I hate that Scott lives on her subway line. I especially hate him for meeting her.

I've been listening to gloomy classical music for a month now. I drag myself to the phone and call the employee assistance program at Peter's company. I've been thinking about doing this for a few days. I explain that I have to go back to work in a week. I can't work though. I can't do much of anything. I think this may have to do with meeting my birth daughter a couple of months ago. A sympathetic male voice is at the other end. He listens to me and tells me that this is a huge life event. Of course I can't complete my sentences without crying. The sympathetic voice says that for me this is 1976 and how for twenty-two years I tucked all this away. He explains that I can't avoid feeling the loss, the regret, the anger. He thinks that I should talk to a therapist, but I can't make another phone call today. This is it. We talk all afternoon. I am feeling better. I turn off the gloomy music. I make dinner. I read to my kids. I make it to work on time.

The train winds through the suburbs of Manhattan. It's Belia's 24th birthday. Up until this morning I wasn't actually sure if I would be spending it with her. In our short time together I have come to know that she is unable to follow through on most plans. It could be her age, but I suspect it is an internal conflict, some sort of betrayal she feels when spending time with me and not her family. I look at the stops with familiarity. I have ridden this line since I was eleven years old. That was the first time I was allowed to go into the city by myself when my mother put me on at the Hartsdale station to meet my father at Grand Central. As we stop at 125th Street, I pull out my makeup bag, brush and mirror. I never feel quite put together so I apply an extra coat of lip-gloss. My stomach is beginning to feel funny. I can't get used to the idea that I am actually seeing my daughter. As we pull into Grand Central, I put my maroon hat on, button up my long navy blue coat then make my way through the station, out the heavy doors and down a very crisp, cold 42nd Street to 3rd Avenue. I am meeting Belia at her office. She is in the lobby, and I give her a hug. She does not hug me the way that my kids hug me. She is reserved, and I am disappointed.

Once in the restaurant, I immediately order a glass of wine. She orders a soda. We begin to settle into a rhythm of conversation as Belia opens the presents that I have for her. I had the idea that I could wrap 24 boxes for each birthday I had missed, but it seemed too much like crazy desperate birth mother thinking, so I settled on less than ten. The dining room is charming and warm with a brick oven for pizza. We dunk the crisp bread into the oil on the table and for a time I feel like her mother. At twenty-four she has a round childlike face, bright brown eyes, toothy smile with a charming giggle.

"I'm going to use the ladies room," Belia says as she stands up.

"Okay," I say and smile.

Looking around I catch the waiter's eye and motion him to the table.

"Today's my daughter's birthday," I say and notice how strange it is to call her my daughter. "Do you have a candle you could put on her dessert?" I ask.

"Of course," he says with a smile.

It's been several minutes, maybe a half hour or an hour since she went to the ladies room. I'm sure she is freaked out and has left, so I order a second glass of wine to keep me company.

170

She finally returns and I'm almost onto a third glass.

"I'm sorry I took so long," she says.

"No problem, is everything alright?"

"Yeah, I had to call my mother and my grandmother. I know they would try to reach me on my birthday," she explains.

"Of course," I say with a forced smile.

Belia told her parents about meeting me. She changed the story. Left the part out that she found me with the bracelet, the bracelet her uncle picked up and saved for her. She knows they don't want to know me. I'm pretty sure they have no idea that she has seen me since our first meeting. But I understand this sharing of time and love. I'm not as good at it as she is though. I keep everyone separate. I could never speak to my mother in the vicinity of Pat. It's too much like cheating. It feels like a betrayal. How can she do it? We finish our little celebration and head back to the train. She insists on walking me to the platform. She is very city savvy, and I appreciate her caring. We hug, say goodbye and I'll call you soon. As I take my seat, I get the same feeling after all of our meetings that I may never see her again. I hold onto the evening to put into the memory bank of my daughter and me.

A spring and summer have passed since our birthday celebration. It is late afternoon on a cool September Saturday, when I pull my Jeep in front of the apartment building off Bailey Avenue in the Bronx. Belia is waiting in front and waves to me. I pull over and she hops in and directs me to a parking spot a few blocks away. I am spending the night. Just the two of us. We drop my stuff off at her apartment and walk to the diner down the block. I give her the Celtic earrings that I bought at the Irish festival earlier in the day. I have a pair similar to hers. We manage to talk endlessly. Never a lull. I want to stop time for a little while. Can we ever catch up, make up, we try. We walk back to her apartment and pick up her car to go grocery shopping. I'm not sure why we are grocery shopping, but I'm happy to be seen out and about with my daughter.

Later I make pudding for her. I'm really bothered by the idea that she has only eaten the kind in plastic cups. The couch is pulled out and we turn on the Miss America Pageant. I know that it won't get any better than this. Lying on the pull out couch, watching Miss America and eating chocolate pudding with my daughter in this little apartment with shiny wood floors, curtains with cute cows and Indian prints. If it weren't for the fumes coming in the window from the Major Deegan, it would be perfect.

The next morning we climb the stairs to the elevated track to catch a movie in Manhattan. I've never ridden on the subway at a point where it's above ground. The train shimmies, as we chat back and forth, not really hearing each other, but chatting all the same. Without warning we come to a complete stop and get tossed from our seats. We are in the middle of what seems to be nowhere underground. I'm thinking this would really stink if we died in here when we are having such a fun weekend. We hold hands, follow the crowd and climb out and up the stairs. I think we are just below Harlem. A line is forming at the corner for a bus. I've had enough adventure for one day. I'll pay. Belia hails a cab. Within seconds we are flying down the West Side Highway as we grab onto anything nailed down to avoid being thrown into the front seat. When we stop in front of the movie theater, I hand the driver a ten and tell him to keep the change. We crawl out of the cab, cross the street, buy our tickets and take the escalators up to the second floor. This is the first movie I've seen with my daughter, so I buy candy, popcorn, diet coke and then we find two seats.

Three seasons have gone since I last saw Belia. Today I watch her make her way down the stairs to the other side of the tracks. Just like my request to Pat, Belia asks to visit the places Scott and I shared so long ago. Our first stop is the house where I grew up. A plain, khaki covered woman answers. I'm not sure if she is old or young, cordial or annoyed. But I think somehow she has been expecting us, as she introduces us to her daughter. She explains that I lived here a long time ago and now I'm showing my daughter. This is where Belia grew in my belly. This is where I got to be her mother. The Khaki covered woman doesn't let us go much further than a few feet in the front door. But I can see that everything is clean, white. A starkness that rose out of the ashes, the pain, the chaos. Everything that was is now gone, made over, redone. Maybe this house was tired of feeling. It can pretend it was always this way. Always clean, always white.

We then drive to the hospital that sits right on the sidewalk. There are no lawns or walking paths. Just another building on the block.

"That's where you were born."

Belia knows the address of the hospital. She and her uncle wrote, pretended to be me and got hold of my medical records. In the end, that is how they found me. My father's signature. His middle initial. It didn't take her long to track him down, send him the letter. I'm still not sure how I feel about them pretending to be me and getting my records. She found me though and that's probably all that matters.

The next stop is Scott's house. I pull in close to the driveway.

"He told me it was a small house. That doesn't look anything like what he described," Belia says.

But it looks just as I remember it. The sunroom takes me back. Her fantasies fade as my memories strengthen.

———————

Belia has become Jewish since I last saw her. She converted for her fiancé. I think this is her second or maybe third engagement. She has a Hebrew name now, Ester, and wants to be buried in Israel. They are Modern Conservatives. I don't understand or really care what it all means. I'm just happy to be able to see her one more time. I've come into the city for dinner and plan to meet her at her office. Originally we were going to meet at Grand Central, but Ester asks if I wouldn't mind coming to the ad agency where she works. I am a bit suspicious by her request. I've suspected that she lies and manipulates. There always seems to be a change of plans or some things just don't seem right, don't add up. But I'll do anything to see her. Scott lives just a block from her office. I'm sure that they have lunch together at least twice a week. The cab and I slither past the nicest apartment in New York, just a peek. I get out at the corner and find the newly renovated industrial turned office building.

The elevator empties into a huge reception area with exposed pipes on the ceiling and cement floors. I let the receptionist know that I'm here for Belia, Ester, I'm not sure who she is here. While I wait, I gaze out the floor to ceiling windows. As she enters, I notice her long skirt, long sleeved blouse and loafers are in contrast to my shorts, tee shirt and sandals. I'm introduced to some of her co-workers, as just Julie. But I think they know who I am. The birth mother, the mother who didn't keep her. As we walk down Sixth Avenue I feel as though I'm on display. Maybe she told Scott I was coming, maybe he's behind us. He's probably not. I can't relax yet. It feels different this time. Everything seems different this time.

I'm happy to get on a cross town bus and out of sight. She has a restaurant in mind. A kosher restaurant. Ester keeps kosher. The restaurant is more formal than I expected. When we take our seats, I drape a napkin over my legs, suddenly feeling quite inappropriate. I was planning on a cheeseburger and a beer. Instead it's the Jerusalem salad and a Manischewitz.

And now she is busy all the time. Our daily phone calls are weekly, then monthly, never. She does not answer my calls, won't return my emails. Silence.

I finally receive a letter. Her handwriting is beautiful, perfect. She thinks we shouldn't see each other or talk for a while. I'm being dumped by the love of my life. I'm going back to the gloomy music, the dark place. Fumbling through the sweaters, I find the box with her letters and cards. Forcing myself to look, read, touch, remember; my shoulders bounce up and down. My limbs are numb as I slip to the floor. These noises are reserved for mourning. I get on with it, go through the motions, push it away, pretend.

And with so much of me focused on Belia, trying to make up for lost time, I'm sure I've neglected my other children. I'll try to be a better mother. I hope it isn't too late.

CHAPTER FOURTEEN

I'VE ALWAYS BEEN AMAZED by Lauren's poetry. Written from a perspective far beyond her years. Some whimsical, some romantic, but most macabre. I could never keep up with her. There were days she would empty her room, put everything in big black garbage bags. Other days she would pile all of the golden books, shelves and shelves of golden books into the middle of her room. Big projects, huge projects, the projects I would never understand. The collage walls carefully constructed with Modgepodge paste, the decorating of the bears, sometimes twenty a day, with hats, jewelry, outfits, hair. I didn't know how to stop her. I didn't think I could. As a young child, blonde hair and bangs, usually a fancy dress and sparkly shoes, she was bubbly and happy. Now she's withdrawn, afraid to leave the house, seems to live in a world that is all her own.

I don't remember what she took the day that initiated the first of more than ten hospitalizations over the next several years. I just remember looking down on us in the admitting office of this lovely estate setting. The trees lining the paths, peaceful, calm, disguising inside the mind of those here, anything but peaceful. Lauren, Peter and me. Me holding an overnight bag. She spent the first night in an observation room of the children's cottage. Alone, no sneakers, nothing she could harm herself with. The other children were much sicker than Lauren, I'm sure of it.

They have lovely buildings and school hours and activities. But they also have punishments. A level system. A system for compliance. She is a sweet girl. It only makes her anxious to think about following the rules and doing her best to be rewarded with a star and rise to the next level. It just makes her retreat more. They say she will get better. How can I leave her here? Why am I leaving her here? I'm doing as I'm told once again. They know better. I'm sure they know better.

The first week, I arrive early for visiting hours. Every moment counts. We'll suffer through this together. We'll get better together.

"When can I come home, Mommy?" Lauren asks.

"Soon honey, soon," I say, knowing it's a lie.

I always make things better. She's too young for me not to make it all better, only eleven, but I leave alone.

Walking down the path from the children's cottage, designed to make it seem like summer camp, I breathe the chilled air as I pass a young boy, probably just eight or nine, surrounded by his parents and an admitting nurse. He must think that his mommy and daddy wouldn't leave him here. And then I recognize the look on the parents' faces. The look that Peter had the first night we brought her here. The night that the psychiatrist told me that because I had given a baby up for adoption, a girl, I had transferred my grief and longing onto Lauren. My fault. The night the social worker learned that Lauren was adopted. That's why. I have to leave my daughter in this place. I will replace my role as mom to that of advocate. Lauren's advocate. Friends will disappear. I don't have time to socialize, their children are fine. What will we talk about? I will begin to withdraw with Lauren. Just the two of us. Peter and I will never agree on what we should do. He is in denial. He doesn't understand her. If she would just go to school. If she would just try an activity, she'd feel better about herself. If she would just stop hiding under the table, if she would just come out of her fantasy life, if she would just stop trying to kill the bugs that are walking up and down her body, then she'd be better.

Our lives have become a system of therapy appointments, psychiatrists, school placement meetings all to make her the way she was. Sean is dragged into this, and I feel the unfairness. He has learned to do his homework under the chairs in the waiting rooms, miss birthday parties and hockey games. In the years to come, he will become the big brother who takes care of her. Driving her, helping her with school and friendships. I have memories of her holding his hand to protect him when they were just toddlers. I miss those days. I knew what to do then. Now I lock her medications away and remove the kitchen knives from the chopping block, hide them. And selfishly the distance between Belia and me comes as a relief.

———

Each night I feel a hand rise up from the floor grabbing mine. Lauren has been sleeping in our room since her diagnosis several months ago. She is afraid I will die through the night if she isn't holding my hand. We've agreed that she can sleep in her sleeping bag next to my side of the bed. Peter doesn't like this new arrangement. He thinks I give into her. But I'm new at having a child with a mental illness. I don't know what is around the corner anymore. Anything that resembles normal is gone, and I'm afraid she's right that I might die and if I don't she might. And within months Peter has left our bed, left our room. left me. And then we will leave each other.

CHAPTER FIFTEEN

I PUT ON MY EMOTIONAL ARMOR and brace for the explosion. I've come to think of Belia's emails as weapons of mass destruction. In between the jokes, inspirations, Amazon shipping confirmation and bank statement, "Belia."

The first in the line of these rapid fire messages was, what I have titled, The Diner. Flanked by her parents, Belia sits with a young man, who she introduces only as her husband. She explains that they are celebrating her parents' anniversary. I wonder how long she has been married and where she lives and how she met him and what his name is, and I know I probably will never know. Our relationship is choreographed by her; her rules, her players, her timing. A few days later the second round; Wedding Pictures. Once again she is flanked by her parents. She is flanked by them in every picture. There is a Catholic priest, so I think she's not Jewish anymore and this guy must not be the Modern Conservative. But the biggest news is that she has a baby girl. She had her just weeks ago. No picture of her though. Only images of Belia dancing with her father on her wedding day.

———————

I want to tell the clerk at Macy's that this soft little pink dress is for my granddaughter. My daughter's daughter. I received a call from Belia this morning. She is in New York. Her husband was recently transferred there. She and the baby are coming. Her husband can't make it.

"I will be driving up this afternoon, so I should be there around four-thirty, five," she tells me.

"Do you remember how to get here?" I ask

"I have a GPS. I'll be fine. I'll see you later," she assures me.

At five o'clock the old pangs of she's not coming creep in. Memories of our broken dates. The birthday celebration I had planned with her. The ice skates had already been wrapped, I waited and waited. She called a few days later to say her father picked her up unexpectedly, took her to her parents' house for a surprise party.

Six, seven o'clock, I'm sure she's not coming. She does; without the baby.

"Gracie has a cold," Belia tells me, passing me quickly through the front door.

"Oh, I'm really sorry. Poor baby," I say turning to catch a quick hug.

Belia looks tiny and thin in the long red cowl neck sweater; much too thin to have just had a baby two months ago. Gone is the young woman I tried to hug in my driveway all those years ago. Now there is an edge to her that is unpleasant and reckless. Her speech, rapid and scattered. She loves Willie Nelson and saw him in Texas. She was sure she would have a boy and she is looking at houses in Greenwich. Her husband is a very successful trader on Wall Street, and she is bathing in what that brings. Her Tiffany wedding rings, the prospect of a house where she can have horses, but her smile doesn't feel genuine. She promises lunch and pictures of the baby. I don't believe her. I don't think I believe she had a baby. But she wouldn't lie about a baby. I feel something's wrong, somewhere in here, and I am positive that this is our final meeting.

Lauren and Sean say hello, but it's been so long since we've spent time together. In the beginning, Belia came to the house several times. We took the kids to the zoo, and I treasure a picture I have of Belia and Lauren in Central Park. But the time never seemed right to tell them who Belia really was, my daughter. Then I was so sure I'd never see her again, but here she is and they are polite to this forgotten friend and she is polite to them as we eat the Chinese food that I picked up three hours ago.

———————

My view of Belia's life continues from a cyber-distance. A quick note with a picture; the picture that tugged at my soul. The second baby, a boy. By the third, I became part of a mass email announcement with a picture of mother and baby, another of grandma, grandpa and big brother around the precious newborn. I feel the assault. The see you weren't included, doesn't it hurt? I am only the birth mother, the bad girl, the one who doesn't deserve to be a part of it.

A year has gone and I've practically forgotten about the baby pictures and announcements, practically. And there it is between Lord and Taylor's Clinique offer and the EZ pass statement, "Belia." Taking cover, I cautiously scan its content. No apologies for not writing sooner, no mention of babies, no pictures, this is different. This is full of anger and resentment and blame rooted in a seething hostility. Belia blames me for all of her unhappiness; every pain she has ever felt. How could I give her away, she doesn't understand. She tells me about the struggles with her parents and how ultimately I am responsible for all of it. How her mother called the state to have her taken away after an all-night high school drinking party.

"Two mothers who wanted to give me away."

I am trembling as I finish the letter that explains her absence from my life over the past several years. My first reaction is to make it all better. I reply immediately. "I'm sorry if I made you feel this way. I love you and will always be here for you." If I tell her I'm sorry then things will change. Maybe then I can see her and the babies. I hit send. But, as her words settle in, my blinded unconditional love turns to anger. I am wounded and so tired of trying. So I have to tell her how I really feel, no sugar-coating, no editing. I email her again. This time the truth. The truth of how I didn't want her family to have her. How I feared her mother's illness, feared the private adoption, the money and the power of the adults around me. The truth that I would never just give her away. And that I thought she wanted me to feel guilt, feel pain for just that. Giving her away.

I hadn't counted on the anger she felt. How for her it hurt to be adopted. I forgot how it hurt to be adopted. I now understood that no matter how much I tried to make it not so, in the end, I was the one who hurt her. I was the one who let her down.

"I'm sorry you didn't get the ending you hoped for," read the closing line of Belia's email.

I am too. The not knowing was easier. The fantasies were richer and kinder.

PART V

Clutter, Critters, the Girls and Mom

CHAPTER SIXTEEN

I CRIED A MONTH TO THE DAY after my father left this earth to take his place in heaven or the clouds or my memory. I wanted to cry before. Thought I should. I didn't, couldn't. The last time I saw him was at the nursing home, alarms hooked to the back of his shirt, leaning forward trying to touch his reality. I didn't know that father. He was someone else, somewhere else. There seemed to be passing moments of clarity, and each time I hoped to catch a glimpse of my dad.

"I'll see you tomorrow Dad. Love you," I whispered as I kissed his cheek.

"Don't leave before you bring me that Pepsi," he called out as I began to walk down the hallway.

He couldn't remember my name, where he was or that my children were almost grown, but he never forgot when I promised him a Pepsi.

"Okay Dad," I nodded.

But I didn't bring the Pepsi. I thought about it, figured he had had enough. Anyway it was almost time for his dinner, when he would begin to become agitated, and besides the aides were with him. So I just kept walking.

———————

White to Main is probably the best route to Green's Funeral Home. I've heard they let the cows out when they made the roads in Connecticut. No grids, just winding roads that may or may not take you where you need to go. Busy place in the morning. I don't drive downtown too often, too many lights, too many cars, too many decaying buildings. Those must be lawyers crossing toward the Courthouse in their dark suits and overcoats, briefcases in tow. Or they may be criminals just trying to look their best, as though this is just a regular day. I didn't choose a dark suit, maybe I should have. The blue blazer and grey slacks are more him. I think I turn left onto main, or is it right? Left at the library. I don't think he ever paid that seven dollar fine he promised to pay for the videos I took out for him. How many years ago was that? There is no need for shoes, you can't see his feet. He can't go barefoot, not with a suit and tie on. I should have brought his black loafers, no his wing tips. The size twelves that took me for rides around the house. "Daddy, can you give me a ride?" The red striped tie should be fine. It will stand out against the white shirt. The blue shirt may have been better. He always looked great in blue.

It was when my father died that my family fell apart. He was the inspiration for our pretense. He was the one we protected, hid, lied about. And though my mother was still here, she was no longer masked by his failures. They were stripped away. The reality of their drinking and destruction showed itself in such ugly ways. The house that once stood prominently at the end of the dirt road, now rotted, abandoned so long ago by disease, anger and resentment.

―――――――――

My mother is perched up by a heap of pillows as she holds court. She has been holding court in her bedroom for years now. It has been established that because of her severe arthritis she can only stand and sit for a limited time. She is very careful to not use up any of her standing or sitting time if it isn't entirely necessary. Usually she holds court with her nightgown on, and a sweater of sorts, always dripping in gold and diamonds. It takes her a few days to do her hair so one may find her tightly set in curlers. She and her Rottweiler, Roxie, nestle in for the better part of each day. There is only enough room for me to stand at the foot of the bed, just shy of blocking the television and a comfortable distance from the Rottweiler's bed, who is kept at bay as my mother lobs biscuits in her direction. This is a sanctuary of sorts. Some notion of normal. My mother's notion, while the rest of the house is infested with dirt, never assembled lamps, night stands, Christmas gifts for the needy, the dogs' pee stains, fresh pee puddles and now rats.

"I'm hearing some critters running around in the attic at night," my mother says, throwing another biscuit to Roxie. "Roxie is bothered by it all night, I think there are squirrels in the attic."

"I'll call an exterminator," I offer.

"No, I will," my mother says as she dismisses me with a wave.

———

The Terminex truck is sitting in front of the garage door as I pull in the driveway of my parents' home. Gary, the exterminator, gets out of the truck, introduces himself and says, "Your dad was a great guy."

"When did you meet my father?" I ask.

"Oh, probably five years ago," he says.

I recall a conversation with my mother when she asked that I do a little research on the internet on how to get rid of rats without actually hurting or killing them. I told her there is no way. So I was quite happy to learn they had called an exterminator.

"Yeah, your dad told me they were good, no more rats," he said.

But that was my father just being my father. He probably didn't see the rats and my mother didn't want to spend the money and ultimately kill them.

As the garage door opens, a haze of decomposing life slams us. I apologize immediately to Gary, who is clearly not as offended by it as I am. I give him a tour of the first floor and though I've known him for under five minutes, I hold onto his arm as I tiptoe anxiously into each new room. He points out the evidence, their droppings and the chewed wires and papers pulled under doors and appliances, the stuffing pulled out on the couches and chairs. I have not studied it all until now. The rats have taken over.

"There are many ways to trap a rat," Gary explains. "But we will not get rid of these rats unless we remove their habitat."

"What do you mean by their habitat?"

"Clutter, furniture, walls. Ah everything. I see this all the time," he tells me. "When people get old, things just go. They say they will clean up, but they don't. I go back every week and set the traps but it's never enough."

And so we agree to try to begin to clear out some clutter.

It's been several weeks since Gary and I first started working together. He thinks I have a future in pest management. We set traps on a regular basis and we have caught a few, but it is becoming clear that this is a futile effort and that something has to give. I pride myself on being able to figure things out. No matter the problem or task, I know I will figure it out. This I can't figure out.

My mother goes downstairs once a day to feed the girls, Roxie and Princess. Princess, a German Shepard mix, has never been upstairs and can be found snuggled on a wicker chair in the family room, surrounded by newspaper for accidents if my mother doesn't get down in time to let her out, which is always. Roxie uses the facilities on the upstairs porch. While the girls have their dinner, she tends to the cat who lives in the garage. Food and water for her and a change of kitty litter, after that she scoops up the seed from the fifty pound bag for the birds. Next it's on to the bread, also for the birds, and the popcorn for the squirrels. Finally she is ready for her lean cuisine, lets the dogs out, waits for them to come in and back to her bed for dessert. She hopes that soon she can move her bedroom downstairs. She is not sure how much longer she will be able manage the stairs.

The last few years of my father's life he was in charge of maintenance. This was not a good idea, really not any idea at all. Whose idea would it be to keep newspapers in the oven, set trash baskets on the top of the stove so the dogs wouldn't get it at night? Who would leave fruit on the counter for weeks, so a bevy of fruit flies could soar through the kitchen? Worse than that, I knew. But there is something in letting your parents have their independence. Something that keeps us in the roles we know. So I have become my mother's complicit, enabling do-gooder. She can't drive any longer, although insists she can. And she can't carry the fifty pound bag of bird seed, the twenty-five pound bag of dog food, ten loaves of bread for the birds and the oversized bags of popcorn for the squirrels. She can't carry the twenty-five pound bag of kitty litter and cases of cat food. She can't get that all by herself, so together we shop for groceries, the animals and hers. Her groceries don't vary. Each week we buy apple sauce so she can put her pill and vitamins in it, skim milk, lean cuisines, only when they are on sale, cheerios, cans of beets, jars of red cabbage and limitless amounts of desserts. Mostly cakes and pies; chocolate pudding cake, lemon cream filled cake, apple pie, strawberry shortcake, lemon meringue pie, low fat ice cream and no fat Cool Whip. It takes about two hours to shop. I have become familiar with the rain check policy, senior citizen discounts and can run circles around the store as my mother hovers over her cart in the bakery section.

We usually make a stop or two before heading home. This has become a bit of a routine for us. I am in the process of a divorce so she takes the time we share to give me unsolicited opinions of working it out, having my twenty-five year marriage annulled, and protecting my assets. I don't interject, and I usually don't listen. Arby's has a sandwich that she likes so we go through the drive thru. She'll have half tonight and the other for lunch tomorrow. Once at the house, I cover my mouth. I can't touch anything. I have to get out before the rats converge. This has become my mountain, my burden, as my mother is blissful, blind and oblivious to what surrounds her.

We began on a sun drenched Saturday afternoon in April. The forty ton dumpster I had rented earlier in the week was set at the edge of the driveway, the closest spot to the house. Four workers, along with Sean and me, suited up with masks and gloves. It was clear from the get go that I was terrified to throw away anything. My mother's grip was so strong that my voice was silenced. But as the day went on, I became unstoppable. As her house was dismantled, she in her bed, Roxie at her side, she grew angrier and angrier; at me.

The first thing we decided was to rip the carpet up. Maybe the smell would ease up. We emptied the big pieces of furniture, placing them on the front lawn, out of my mother's view. Her window was directly over the dumpster so we couldn't easily get rid of things.

"I don't want anyone to throw away my Christmas stuff," she yelled from the window. "Dammit, don't throw out the globe!"

Our crew became slyly skilled in tossing the debris. The horror would continue for weeks as walls came down, cabinets removed, floors torn up, the attic and basement emptied all in an effort to rid the rats. It would take ten forty ton dumpsters to make a dent. And through it all, my mother couldn't understand. She would hand me lists each time I saw her.

Items that are missing:

Dog vitamins
Plastic cover for microwave dinners
Tasha (well, Tasha's ashes)
Crossword puzzle books

I had hoped she would see the gravity of the situation and want to move, but she wouldn't leave. With time she thought she would like a new kitchen and to move her bedroom downstairs. I still couldn't picture it. This was going to take time. Time I wasn't sure we had. Her body and mind were slipping away.

———————

"Help me. Help me," a faint voice mutters. I'm not sure what I hear. I run up the stairs two at a time, but it feels like I am not getting there fast enough. My heart racing and hands shaking, I open the door to see my mother on the floor, her legs under the bed, in her own excrement, barely able to speak.

Several weeks ago, I had threatened to call Social Services and the ASPCA, which of course would have been the smart and responsible thing to do. But I am frozen when it comes to my mother. I let her call the shots, no matter the cost, and now she is near death. Seventy over thirty; do people live with their blood pressure that low? A bleeding ulcer. The worst they have ever seen, right next to her main artery. I should have done something sooner.

So while my mother is in and out of surgery, intensive care and on her tenth blood transfusion, I am left to deal with her house and her animals. The cleanup continues. I've become much braver around the rats and the traps. The clutter isn't just clutter anymore; there are years of memories, my father's clothes and jewelry of my mother's that I'm sure she has long forgotten. I'm reminded of my father's mission as Eucharistic minister, when I found a lone communion host. As the years slipped by and his dementia worsened, he would take several hosts, about a week's worth, from the tabernacle in the chapel of the church. He'd pull his big red van with the "I Love God" license plate onto the walkway of the church's side entrance, crushing anything in its path, get the hosts and bring them home. He and my mother would have communion each morning as they watched the Mass on Channel 21. And there he was, Jesus, under the cheerios, old yogurt containers and six year old Women's Day magazines. I did the only thing I could, place Jesus on my tongue and make the sign of the cross.

CHAPTER SEVENTEEN

THE DOGS HAVE MOVED IN WITH ME. Now I have four. I've thought from time to time, usually when I'm holding Roxie back from attacking someone, if I had gone to Shoprite before checking in on my mother, it may have been too late. And then I scold myself for such a thought and call a dog trainer. For $3,000 he will cure this Rottweiler of years of aggression. So I put it on my credit card and off she goes.

My mother is getting stronger, but after she spends several weeks at the rehabilitation center, she doesn't have a home to return to. It's not habitable. Not yet anyway. I'm still trying to figure it all out. For now she will take my room, with the bathroom just off of it. I will sleep in Sean's room, who's away at college. Princess, my mother's Shepard mix, has taken the living room; she and her fur will not go anywhere else. Peter, now my ex-husband, is back with us living downstairs since his company went under, and Lauren is having breakdown after breakdown in the room next to my mother.

The latest plan is to remodel my mother's house, sell mine, and the kids and I will live with her. I absolutely hate the idea, but I'm thinking about my financial future now that I am single and this could be cost effective.

I know that if anyone is actually going to live there, most everything must be replaced. I hire an architect to configure a new kitchen, make four bedrooms out of five, enlarge existing bathrooms, move doorways all in the name of my mother will have her space and I will have mine. Demolition must be done, electrical replaced. The three season room has to be torn down before it falls down, damaged by years of the Rottweiler frequenting its roof.

It all sounds good, but as my mother becomes stronger and more herself, it's becoming clearer and clearer that we are not going to be able to share a house. She likes things her way and she doesn't like to spend money. I cannot convince her that Clorox cannot fix the kitchen cabinets and the bathrooms and that the porch has to go. I try to keep the entire scope of the construction as my problem, to ease her anxiety as my anxiety escalates. After a visit to the house with my niece, she sees it in its demolition stage and is now convinced that it will be like this forever. And we are through. Somehow I am responsible for all of this.

I hoped to return to a better time. When my parents first moved in. After the fire. After the fights. After the darkness. A fresh start, again. So the grandchildren could come and visit and swim in the pool. But then I had forgotten that it was my father who was the one who enjoyed the grandchildren and the pool. In my fantasy, my mother would sit on a shaded deck and have company and live a happy life. She in the lovely apartment we'd create just off the family room, Lauren, Sean and me in the rest of the house. Our house would be spectacular. A house with a fireplace and grill in the kitchen, open ceilings, beautiful new bathrooms, new entrance, new life, new beginning. But instead I have ruined her house and her life and she won't leave my bed because she has no place to go. So week after week, month after month she stays and slowly she strips me of my duties as power of attorney, trustee of my father's will, and my bedroom is looking more like her bedroom, with cakes and pies and cheerios, a small refrigerator, rosary beads, magazines and powder on the floor.

——— ———

"Lauren, please open the door," I say as calmly as I can pretend.

We just left the psychiatrist's office no more than ten minutes ago, who determined that Lauren could not agree to keep herself safe.

"Mom, can we just stop home, so I can get a book and a change of clothes?" Lauren asks.

"No, Lauren they are holding a bed in Norwalk for you."

"Please Mom, I'll just be a minute. I promise. I really just want to get my stuff. It will make me feel better."

So I pull into the driveway and within moments I find myself at her door, pleading with her to come out.

I should have known better.

I call the psychiatrist and let her know what I just fell for.

"She needs to go to the hospital. You have to insist," she directs me.

But with Lauren I don't always get it right. By the time Sean and I get her door open, she is in her closet, hands firmly wrapped around a pole, dug in.

Entering Lauren's room, my mother hands me the phone. She always picks it up on the first ring. The phone is next to her bed, my bed.

"It's the doctor," she tells me, then adds, "The girls are coming over tonight for pizza and bringing the kids."

"Mom it's really not a good night. Lauren is in her closet, I have to get her down to Norwalk Hospital before they give her bed away. Another night," I say, covering the phone.

"Oh, they won't be any trouble. We'll just stay in the kitchen," Jenny is off tonight so it's the only time they can come," she adds.

Lauren has been hospitalized twice since my mother's arrival. Lauren's mental illness has never been something my mother could understand. She's sure that if Lauren didn't insist on being an Atheist and just put herself in Jesus's hands she would be fine. Lauren's on to her third hospitalization, so I have to choose my obligation. My mother or my daughter.

I have to get my mother to move somewhere. I suggest a myriad of possible solutions, an assisted living facility.

"I can't, they don't accept dogs over twenty-five pounds."

So I try again with a condo.

"I can't afford that."

And by my fifth suggestion it is clear she is not going anywhere.

The attorney's office is located in the next town.

"I need to get my mother out of my bed," I say. "My daughter's mental health is being seriously affected."

"We can send her attorney an eviction notice. She will have thirty days to vacate," he says in a strictly matter of fact tone.

"There is no other way?" I ask.

"That really is it," he tells me.

"Alright then," I say and we start the paperwork.

My sister, Dianne, has come through. I called her the other day and without a hello, blasted her for ten minutes for having to do everything myself and now it was her turn. According to her, my mother never wanted her coming into her house, so she didn't. My brothers escaped to the midwest years ago, only to be heard from every fifth Christmas. Over the past several months, no years, I have felt like an only child. I am the oldest, and so I do what I have to. But I can't do it anymore. This new alliance with my sister has allowed me to begin to look beyond the hopelessness. Dianne is looking for emergency housing. My mother is convinced that despite my father's pension, social security, stocks and bonds she is destined to the streets or at least a seedy motel, where she insists my sister take her. Instead Dianne brings her to a lovely independent living facility that she has already checked out and has cleverly offered as a temporary place.

"Just try it out, for the summer, Dianne begins. "It's light and airy. A cleaning staff will come once a week. You can have dinner in your apartment or in the dining room, there are games and movies and.."

She hates it. She will only take it out of desperation.

The following weekend we meet at my mother's house with a U-Haul to gather the few things that can be cleaned up to make her feel more at home in her new place. We can't tell her what we are doing, she will not allow it and another month will come and go and the eviction thing will be even messier. It takes us all day and into the evening, but we have her new apartment looking as though she has been there all along.

It's been less than a week since the move, and I'm visiting my mother at the independent living facility. This is one of the first truly warm spring afternoons we've had all season, so we put a couple of chairs outside by the door under a willow tree. Drinking iced tea, she tells me about the people she has met and the cat who comes to visit her. I think she may secretly like it here. She thinks that it's too far to walk to the dining room and activities each day, but I'm happy she's thinking about going at all. After spending the afternoon, I kiss her goodbye and tell her I'll visit again soon. As I drive away, we wave, and for the first time since forever I know she is safe. But I fear we may have lost each other in the process.

PART VI

Stories, Seafood, Ave Maria and
Grandma Mary

CHAPTER EIGHTEEN

AUGUST WILL SOON FLOW INTO SEPTEMBER, with the deep green fading from the leaves. Today I'm meeting Pat's mother, my grandmother. The grandmother who was described by the adoption agency as a stern woman. The drive to her apartment in Maine should take me close to four hours. I'm excited to have an adventure ahead of me as I back the car out of my driveway, CD's and cooler with bottled water set conveniently on the passenger's seat, E-ZPass in place and the box of chocolates I bought this morning at Bridgewater Chocolates. I know I can't go wrong with a five pound box tied with a ruby red velvet ribbon.

In the beginning of my relationship with Pat, I had hoped to meet her parents. I felt surely they would love me. I missed my grandparents who I had grown up with and thought I could have another chance for unconditional love. Pat didn't tell them that she had found me though. It was too tricky for her, and I was probably just being selfish. But on a Christmas night, when everything had been opened and eaten, dishes done, Pat and her mother settled in for the evening to watch television. A pregnant teenager was talking about the challenges she faced.

"I should have stood by you. I should have been there for you," her mother said.

"I've met her," Pat began.

Jumping from the couch, she collected the scrapbook of my perfect life. They sat closer than they had in years, sharing the loss for the first time. Remembering the baby, meeting the child, the teenager, the bride, the mother.

———

Now as I cross the bridge from New Hampshire into Maine, I immediately feel connected, maybe to the earth, maybe to the past. Rolling down the windows, the air is warm and salty. The highway is dotted with cabins, convenience stores and pine trees. I make a call to Pat's cell to let her know I'm just a few miles away. I can hear she's nervous. Driving through the town, larger than I expected, I see the church that is my landmark and turn right. One block down I come to the apartment complex for seniors. The three story buildings are dotted with park benches and winding walkways. I park in the lot closest to Building F and take a deep breath.

Balancing my large green duffle and box of chocolates, I find the buzzer for apartment 3F. Once inside the lobby, a white haired lady, mail in hand, stops me to ask who I am visiting.

"Mary O'Connor," I tell her.

"Are you her granddaughter?" she asks.

I don't answer her, I'm not sure what the correct answer is, so I smile and push the button for the elevator.

"Oh, she is on the third floor. She may have some mail in her box, would you take it to her?"

"Sure," I agree.

Stepping off the elevator, I see Pat opening the door. She gives me a quick hug hello. I drop my bag and hand her the mail and the chocolates. The living room is just feet away, and I'm sure I recognize everything in it. The floral couch and wingback chair, the early American hutch that holds the Franciscan china and the TV tray in front of the rocking chair where Grandma Mary sits. Bending over, I give her a hug.

"I'm so sorry my husband insisted. That was the way it was then," she tells me through a broken voice and a lisp.

"Please, don't be upset. I'm happy and have a good life. I know how hard it was then," I assure her.

I can see the tears she was holding back. I can feel her chest pound, her stomach wave, and finally understand her heartbreak. Ninety-three and I'm sure she still remembers that taxi ride to the adoption agency. Three generations; severed by shame and timing and broken dreams on a hot, sticky July afternoon a lifetime, my lifetime ago.

Breaking away from our hug, I sit on the couch as close to her as I can get and show her the pictures of my children. I've also brought pictures of my parents, and she is sure she has seen my father before. Perhaps she has. With that out of the way, I begin to ask her questions about her life and family and suddenly I am a child again, hanging on to every word as images come alive of a time long ago. Pat interrupts us to go to dinner, knowing that we would sit here for hours and hours talking about Yonkers and basketball, giggling about mothers in-law and comparing our feet and skinny ankles.

I'm happy that we are going to a seafood restaurant. A seafood restaurant in Maine, and I'm feeling like I'm on vacation. Grandma Mary uses a cane, but I think it's mostly for show. I'm struck by her amazing agility. I'm sure I see a bounce in her step; I can feel one in mine.

216

At the restaurant, we are seated at a table in a cozy room with wood floors and walls with seafaring paintings.

"May I get you ladies something to drink?" the waitress asks as she hands us our menus.

"Do you have Sam Adams on tap?" Grandma Mary asks.

"I'll have the same," I add.

Pat orders a white wine spritzer as Grandma Mary and I give each other a knowing look.

Giggles, beer on tap, fried mushrooms and the catch of the day; it's Grandma Mary I take after, Grandma Mary.

CHAPTER NINETEEN

St. Mary's looks too large to sit on this corner. It needs a setting. Rolling hills with cherry blossoms in bloom. But instead it holds its breath to fit on a lot in downtown Yonkers. Pat called me a week ago to tell me that her mother had died. Grandma Mary. I only met her that one time. But for me, it was so perfect that we were meant only to have those two days. The memory would be enough. I'm sure Grandma Mary thought that too.

I was hoping that I could just sit in the back and go unnoticed. I know Anthony and Lisa, my other sister. I finally met Lisa when Pat told her brother Jack (now Uncle Jack) about me. He never knew. None of her brothers knew. Then Pat decided to have a lunch and invite him and Lisa and Anthony and Anthony's family and me. I loved Lisa and Jack instantly. I mostly love Lisa's laugh. She has a laugh that stretches out and hugs you. And Uncle Jack is sweet and kind, and I know he is happy to have this new niece. But as I enter the church there are people I don't know, some that I think look just like Pat and may not know about me. Her two other brothers still don't know I exist and this is their mother's funeral, but I can't hide. So I sit in a pew just a few rows down from the altar. There are readings, one by her great granddaughter and Lisa does the eulogy. Ave Maria makes everyone cry and then there are smiles for this woman who lived close to ninety-eight years.

After the mass, Pat gives me a hug and insists I come to the cemetery and lunch to follow.

"Does everyone know who I am?" I ask.

"Well not everyone. I told my cousin last night. My brother James isn't talking to anyone anyway. It's fine," she says.

I parked just down the block and don't want to get lost going to the cemetery, so I ask Uncle Jack if I can follow him closely.

Nearing my car, I feel a tap. A man. He must be one of Pat's brothers. He looks a bit like Uncle Jack.

"Hi I'm Ken," he says as he shakes my hand.

"I'm Julie."

"I'm Pat's brother."

"I'm Pat's daughter."

"I just heard," he says shaking his head.

Then we part ways and quickly get in our cars and follow the procession.

The cemetery is probably fifteen minutes away from the church, and I think we've driven on at least two parkways. But I manage to keep up. It's a beautiful May Saturday and it feels good even here at the cemetery. I stand behind Uncle Jack, but feel all eyes on me. Maybe I shouldn't have come. This is their time.

Before I can change my mind, "Julie, you are coming to the restaurant," Uncle Jack insists.

And so it's been decided.

Close to thirty of us squeeze around a long lone table with Italian food, set in a long lone room off an Italian restaurant. The uncle who I just met today is seated at the head of the table, his wife next to him. The cousins are at the other end. I try to sit next to Lisa, who I hope can shield me from any awkward stares, but instead I sit next to Courtney. Courtney is seven years old and just learned a few days ago from her father, my brother Anthony, that I am her aunt.

So while the table of relatives toast to Mary's long life, Courtney yells to Pat, "Grandma, how come I never knew I had an Aunt Julie?"

"Because Courtney, we saved the best for last."

And then we pass around the large plates of antipasto.

221

EPILOGUE

FORTY AUTUMNS HAVE PASSED since my sophomore year of high school. Some flew, some stood still, some a blaze in color, others grey. But always welcomed after the hot and humid days of summer. We did get out of Vietnam, then went to war in other countries for reasons I still can't understand. Wars are no longer the lead story, the news is now on twenty-four hours a day and Roe v. Wade has become a political divide in the nation. Last year, Carole King did an oldies tour and Elton John and his husband had their second child. I don't smoke, and you can't find TAB anywhere, but I do have a hard time passing up the Kit Kats at the checkout line.

Belia and I could never seem to connect. We somehow got in the way. I received another email and she announced that she was bringing her children to see Scott later that week. So she sees Scott. Yes, she sees Scott. A few years ago I would have been shattered by the idea. Now I hope she can find peace with the circumstances of her birth, her adoption. And Scott, I think he still has that fabulous apartment in Chelsea, and I'm sure he's still good looking, and he gets to see Belia and the grand babies. And someday I will let go of this, really. I thought that's where it ended, but just last week I received word from Belia. This time the love whispered through and my heart opened and maybe, maybe this time. Love is like that.

Pat and I have maintained a loving friendship. It's one of those where six months can go by when we finally talk, and it feels like no time at all. She is almost old, and lives in Florida most of the year. She turns her cell phone off and doesn't use email, she only wants to paint and play tennis without the drama she leaves behind in New York, and I love that about her.

Peter got cancer. Everyone shows up when you get cancer. He's fighting the fight and we are helping him in every way we can. Sean is getting him a new cap for when he starts chemo again. He brought the first one to him from Peru where he spent a semester. Lauren keeps him laughing and reminds him of all of his doctors' appointments, and I am wading through the paperwork. We have an unusual divorce. Some think it's crazy, others envy it. I think it's modern. He finally moved across the river. He comes home once in a while, and somehow we have managed to stay a family.

I saw my mother on Easter Sunday at my niece's house. She slowly made her way into the living room, cane in one hand, granddaughter in the other, eyes cast down because of the arthritis. "Mom why don't you sit here," I offered. She slowly tilted her head; a beautiful smile came across her face when she realized it was me. "I didn't know you would be here, come give me a kiss."

ACKNOWLEDGMENTS

THIS BOOK BEGAN ITS JOURNEY long before I could have known there was a story to be told. Memories, musings, recollections of day to day experiences strewn about, somehow found their way to form this memoir. I have come to understand that I am both player and reporter of these events. It is in the reporting that I owe immense gratitude to the people who taught, supported and encouraged me. Lauren Slater was the first to support me in the idea that this indeed was a story worth telling. She and Karen Propp chiseled the original clay that was my writing, revealing a tale, still in its infancy. To the women around the conference table at the Yale Writer's Workshop; without your critiques, suggestions, encouragement and friendship; this book would not be a complete work. I am forever grateful to Tom Murphy, Lauren Kerton, Trish Lynch, Denise D'Andrea Boffi and Rick Bause for their generous gift of time and attention while proofreading and copyediting the manuscript. Like most everything in my life, I couldn't do it if it weren't for the love and support of my amazing family and friends, too many to name, but none forgotten. And to Melissa and Debbie; I'll see you at Pee Wee's beach house in August.

ABOUT THE AUTHOR

JULIE KERTON IS AN ACTIVE contributor on adoption issues, including hosting her blog, shenamedyoudonna.blogspot.com. She is a strong proponent of adoption reform, pertaining to the civil rights of Adult Adoptees. In addition she advocates for families affected by mental illness and is a member of NAMI (National Alliance on Mental Illness). Julie holds a B.S. in Human Development and Psychology and lives in Connecticut.

CPSIA information can be obtained at www.ICGtesting.com
Printed in the USA
BVOW07s0427170215

387960BV00002B/76/P